FUSION OF REALITY

K. VARIA

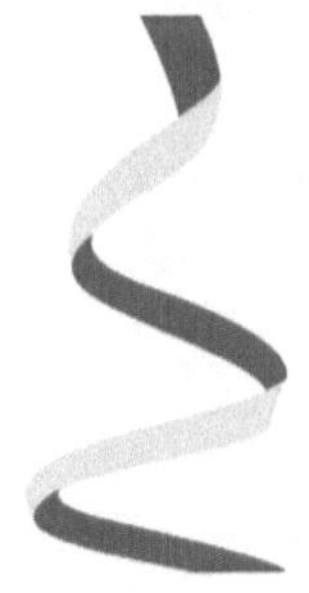

KINETIK SOLUTIONS

LONDON

Fusion of Reality
© 2025 K. Varia

Published by Kinetik Solutions Ltd.

ISBN: 978-0-9932390-5-2

For enquiries, visit fusionofreality.com

Dedicated to:

My soulmate, Kaku.

My mother, Aruna, who lived by the strength of meaningful relationships.

My grandmother, Shantaben, whose wisdom remains my guiding light.

And the Jain monk, Amar Muni, whose words give me strength.

Acknowledgements

Many people read drafts of this book, offering their time, insights, and encouragement. I will always remain grateful to them for their thoughtful feedback and support. Thank you to:

Alba Gros Santasusana, Alicia Carchedi, Anant Shah, Anne Taylor, Chloe Haimes, Danny Sansom, Dhruvi Punjani, Diogenes Angelides, Duncan Jarrett, Jake Eiseman-Renyard, Jayni Gudka, John Morgan, Jonna Byskata, Karelisa Hartigan, Kruti Varia, Lauha Fried, Lisa Cunningham, Lucy Green, Maureen Malden, Nadia David, Peter Karran, Richard Gold, Richard Simon, Saadath Ali, Saima Miah, Sally Kimberley, Sangita Shrestha, Sanjiv Bhardwaj, Shital Shah and Tasha Staunton.

Special thanks to the Editing and Publishing Support Team for their invaluable dedication:

Ariba Baig, Caroline Appleby, David Williams, Gautam Pujari, Lily Bushell, Louise McGuinness, Sanya Sowani and Tesni Adams.

Sensitivity Reading: Sanyukta Shrestha

Cover Design: Matthew Rudhall

Typesetting: Simon Hough

CHAPTER 1

UP AND AWAY

Last night, Grandad appeared in my dreams, like he does on big occasions. He was lecturing me, but I can't remember the words. On his head was a dark green and blue chequered Nepalese *ṭōpī*.

Toothbrush in hand, I walk up and down the top-floor landing. Today is my most important meeting at DigiArt, my fourth job since graduation. Despite the politics, backstabbing and the artificiality of relationships, my other home is the corporate world.

My wife Mona's voice floats up from the kitchen. She may be the calmest in our family, but not when arguing with our son Nabin. 'Don't forget your lunch. You forgot it twice last week. It's not —' Before I can poke my head down, the front door slams shut. The patter of Nabin's quick steps on the pavement enters through the bedroom window.

I find my indigo suit, which has a lavender smell from the dry-cleaning, and my hardly worn copper green tie. With my hair gelled, I like what's in the mirror. Yet the corners of my lips are a little downturned. Since I started work, promotion meant everything to me, yet every rise up the ladder made me anxious, and I couldn't understand why. I look up at the loft hatch. My plan for the conversion will fit in perfectly with the salary uplift if I get the promotion. I clench my right fist and pat my thigh twice.

The front door latch opens and closes with a little click. There is no electric hum from Mona's car. Has the overnight charge failed? I am by the top of the stairs when the latch chinks again. Orange light enters the front door, seeping into the hallway.

'Good luck with your meeting, Aman. Hope it goes well!' Mona says.

I bend down to see her ultramarine skirt in the doorway. 'Thanks, you know how much this means to us …' Before I can say any more, the light is gone. The synthetic purr of her BMW drifts away.

***

The top-floor office next to the boardroom annexe has a Renaissance-themed clock. The large hand with the factory-made engraving is at 10. Underneath, the whiteboard displays the words: *Right Strategy Means Opportunity.*

I crafted these words for the product strategy workshop last week. My shoulders drop back. I am glad no-one has wiped away my thoughts, pressed into the board with the electronic stylus. The hair in my nose twitches. The room has a hint of cheese. No doubt, one of the directors has used it for breakfast combined with a call to the East.

The four fluorescent lights, arranged diagonally, are blinding. My skin is tingling. I look at the large clock hand and try to make out its movement. The tick is fainter than the tock.

The last time I felt in knots was on a video call with the doctor. That was six months ago.

Both engraved hands on the clock are together, pointing up. Peter walks in. His shining head makes his clean-shaven face look rounder and his ears bigger. My boss is just under six feet tall, three inches taller than me. His stomach is flat; he has grey-blue eyes and a perfect nose. I push my left hand through my sticky hair. The one thing I have over him is the full crop on my head.

He has the same tiny smirk as when he requested this meeting, but this time carries a beige A4 envelope, which he places upside down on the table. We have an office policy that says: *Print on exception*. My guess is that there are at least ten pieces of paper from its thickness. Peter's suit fits him just right on his shoulders and is embellished with a blue and green tie. His slim body settles down into the large, padded chair. His first gaze is side to side on my shoulders.

He says, 'I like the colour of your tie. How's the family? All in splendid health?'

I stroke my tie, like I am trying to wipe out the green. His pace is in rhythm with each tock. He must have prepared his lines.

'Let me get straight to the point, Aman. We like your strategic ideas, and the workshop last week made me realise some opportunities we'd missed. Your innovation in digitising and marketing Renaissance art has worked well. I have spoken to the senior leadership team, and we want to offer you the position of Head of New Products as part of our strategic plan. The salary increment is 17% and you start on ...'

I stop listening. A bull clip grips my heart, and moisture is in my armpits. The smell of lavender from my suit is much stronger. I want to leap up, but I shuffle in my seat thrice. In my last job, my ideas on digitising art for creative spaces and fashion were openly laughed at.

Peter's words drift back, 'I want you to head up a new team. Together, you can develop new opportunities that DigiArt has with the Cloud-based platform for licensing art.'

I have rehearsed my answer in many daydreams: 'I am humbled to be given this opportunity. You know my commitment to the organisation and its goals.'

He nods, turns the envelope around and pushes it forward. It says in neat handwriting: *Aman Pradhan – Head of New Product Development*. He shakes my hand, turns 90 degrees and walks to the door without glancing back. His left eye narrows, and his mouth tightens.

Immediately, I walk to the bathroom; my heart still beats at full speed. I stand over the urinal, going over the whole meeting again. The envelope is under my arm. I pat my chest with my left hand. Many times, self-doubt nagged me about the clever business phrases I articulated. But today, they make complete sense to me. The bathroom door makes a low-octave thud. I zip up. It's the technician from the second floor. I can tell from the printed T-shirt and the stonewashed jeans. I avoid eye contact.

For the rest of the afternoon I daydream, predicting the future with challenges I will likely encounter. I visualise our loft conversion with a ping-pong table and a mini cinema. The winter light seems brighter through the open-plan office window.

My best friend Raff once asked me, 'Aman, is your work meaningful?' I like Raff's challenges, but his question was nonsensical.

As soon as I get in my car, I call him. He picks up after one ring.

'Hi Raff, so sorry not to have contacted you to arrange squash. I have been drowning in work. I wanted to share some good ...'

He cuts me off. I put on my seatbelt. Raff's ordinarily deep voice is in a higher octave.

He says, 'Listen, I have had to take Sunita to Chase Farm Hospital more times than I thought. Worse than that, my daughter hasn't called since last week despite leaving two messages.'

I run my hand over the wood-panelled interior of my two-year-old Mercedes EQB 250+. When Raff's feeling down, he always exaggerates how strained things are with his daughter. I promise to meet him at the weekend, but at the second set of traffic lights, I see the sign for Enfield. It's where Raff lives. My heart throbs and guilt rises from my gut. The driver behind me hoots as I make a left turn without putting on my indicator. I switch on my satnav as my tummy settles. I arrive thirty-five minutes later outside no. 71

and smile at the sight of the blue knocker. Raff hugs me and then his small, puffy hand shakes mine three times.

As I enter the living room, Sunita shouts, her voice full of energy, 'Aman, so nice to see you.' I look closely at her face. She sits up straighter. Her voice goes down an octave. She says, 'This stupid disease, it's not going to get the better of me!'

Pictures of their daughter are on one side of the room. Sunita's face is serene and her shoulders are up, but then I am not a doctor. A little later, she confirms my intuition. She says, 'At the last visit they said the drugs are working and the consultant is pleased with the progress.'

Forty minutes later, Raff steps outside the front door as I leave. The latch clicks; he comes nearer. His grey pupils are mesmerising. He says, 'Listen, I have had to relook at my life with Sunita's illness.'

I want to tell him about my promotion.

'I am going to quit my job and take the opportunity to be a college teacher. Do you remember I did the PGCE post-uni? From what I can see, the pay will be atrocious. But it will mean more time to sort out my domestic situation. Anyhow, I will enjoy developing the next generation.'

There is no point talking about my uplift now. Raff won't acknowledge it in the way I'd want. 'Makes no sense, Raff. It's taken you twenty years to get to this position. Another ten years, and you can retire and do what you want. You might even get a payoff as a future director. You are lucky you have a team of twenty-five who work to your will. Plus, you don't have the pressures of selling at all in renewable infrastructure.'

Raff adjusts his rectangular brown glasses upwards and looks up at the solar-panelled roof on the opposite house. That tells me he doesn't want me to argue. At least, not right now. I wonder if I could take over Raff's job and increase my salary. Five heartbeats later, my right fist tightens. I want to hit myself for such an indulgent thought.

Still, Raff is making a rash decision. His wife has access to the best doctors, and the family's troubles will get sorted; running away from a prime job is not the right answer.

My euphoric feeling returns on meeting the first traffic light on my way home. I go through what Peter said again, searching for hidden information in the words he used.

At home, Nadia, my daughter, is standing at the top of the stairs. I crank my head up.

She doesn't start with a hello. 'Dad, the television image is terrible today. I can't watch *Bake Off for Teens*. It's been like that for weeks. When are you going to fix it?'

'Definitely this weekend. Maybe Saturday ...'

Before I can say more, I hear loud, high-pitched noises from the kitchen. It's the sound of Nabin and Mona arguing. The most common words are 'lunch,' 'forget' and 'waste.' I shake my head. Completely predictable. Nabin never forgets his football gear on Saturday or the humongous salaries of Premier League players.

I remove my tie and throw it on my bed. I jump on our Duxiana mattress and switch on the music player on my phone; I want to preserve my high mood for as long as possible. I ask my AI app for *exclusive ten-day breaks in Dubai*. It's what I promised the family if I got the promotion. Pictures of Palm Jumeirah on Instagram bring me instant pleasure. I keep scrolling, my excitement heightened by a drone shot one hundred metres up, showing a pristine beach with palm trees lined up like a highway.

Half an hour later, there is the sound of chatting in the living room. It's my chance to announce my big news.

'What does digital art strategy actually mean?' Nabin asks. 'Does this mean you get more money?'

People say Nabin looks like me, but I think he looks like my dad; his chin is more jutting. But then, Nabin has just turned twelve.

Mona looks at Nabin and breaks into a giggle. During my last promotion two years ago, I explained the correlation between promotion and cash.

Nadia's eyes show not even a flicker of interest. But then they never have. She turns to Nabin, waves her thin fingers and gossips about someone at school she dislikes.

Mona is leaning sideways next to me; her eyelids are drooping. Today was her nine-hour stint at the hospital.

'Digital art will be a market leader in several new industries. The main thing is building partnerships with platform providers across the globe. I mean, there is a real possibility of getting to the very top here.' I see Nabin's blank face, shake my head and laugh. 'Sorry about the gobbledygook; I was just saying digitised art is in big demand, and I like it.'

Mona taps my hand. Her mother gave us a loan of £14,000 for my MBA studies. I told my mother-in-law that the investment would make me thrive within five years. I want my family to gush at me for at least another ten minutes. Instead, I pat my chest twice and start dreaming about the future.

Nadia stands up, unlocks her phone and sits on the sofa ledge beside me. She holds her hand out and shows me an Instagram post. My dream stops instantly. It's Kaya, her hair braided back, in a pink dress showing her engagement ring, her hand placed across her shoulder. It's a floral pattern embossed on gleaming gold.

There is sweat on my palms. Kaya's wedding is less than a year away

Nadia comes closer. 'Dad, how's the planning going? I heard from Kaya that you're managing it all.'

After my niece's engagement was announced two months ago, I put my hand up. It's what my sister expected. My exact words to Kaya were, 'I run mega projects at work. This will be easy. Please don't go to a wedding planner.'

Anyway, I love Kaya as much as my daughter. I used to see her many times a week after she was born, and this only diminished after Nadia became a part of my life.

For the wedding, or project as I see it, I have done little so far. I need to speak to Kaya, and soon.

Nadia opens her round palm, moving it towards me. 'Are we going to a country estate or the function hall? Will Uncle Lekh be involved in the organising?'

Lekh is my first cousin. When I was ten, we started to go to the *Bāhā*, a Buddhist temple, with my grandad for sermon and meditation. On top of that, Lekh and I shared two common bonds: the time we spent together playing competitive games and the number of times we went to the chip shop. Everyone mistook us for brothers. Most importantly, as kids, we shared the experience of our fathers' frequent quarrels. We never discussed their disputes and pretended they never happened.

I had avoided Lekh since our fallout seven years ago. We got on well while growing up in Aldershot, but our last conversation was brutal. He had refused point-blank my request for the loan I wanted for my MBA. After that point, things went downhill. Now, Lekh and I don't argue like our dads used to; we just don't speak.

I push Lekh out of my mind and replay my meeting with Peter, reliving the moment he pushed the envelope towards me.

We all move into the kitchen. Mona gazes at the empty table.

'Hope you got the tomatoes?'

Nadia giggles. She shakes her head three times and then closes her eyes.

'Huh? I don't believe it. Did you not see my message?'

I want to say it was my intention to get some fresh tomatoes at lunchtime, but I had automatically gone to the coffee shop instead. I blurt out, 'Sorry.'

My wife turns her back to me and puts the gas flame on higher.

During dinner, I explain what NFT means, wanting my family's attention.

Nabin nods like he understands but he is playing with the fettuccini, turning it round and round.

Mona yawns. The moment we all finish she is up.

She turns around from the dishwasher. 'I hope you can get Lekh involved. Having the whole family mucking in will be helpful.'

For my wedding, cousins appeared out of nowhere to help. In Newar culture and within the traditions of people of the Kathmandu Valley, weddings are much more than just a union between the bride and groom. They are a matter of family pride. For those of us who are also Buddhist by birth, weddings also serve as an acknowledgement of a higher purpose. My grandad drummed that into me. My dad and Lekh's dad had put their differences aside for my wedding, only to pick them up again once everything was over.

My forehead is hot. My fingers release the dirty dishes. There is a vibrating thud as they hit the table. Mona's eyes open wide. I take a step back and yell, 'Why are you all talking about Lekh? Please leave this wedding to me. We don't need anyone else.'

Mona turns her back. The taps come back on, making a sound like a wave hitting the shore. That calms me. I wipe the table as the kids put things away in the fridge. The phone rings. All three stop and twist their necks at me.

I don't even bother checking who it is. It can only be Kaya, and I instantly press the red button and turn the phone upside down. Mona turns back and looks at the flower on the windowsill. She does not blink.

I feel tension in my stomach. Kaya will have many questions to which I have no answers. I deduce that Kaya must have already spoken to the rest of my family about the wedding preparations. Telling Kaya that work consumes me would be shameful.

My wedding was lovely, but now it takes a while to remember all the facts. Mona was born into a Hindu family, her mum Burmese and her dad Nepalese. Her parents were non-practising. But, by the time we met, she had dabbled in Eastern philosophies and meditation. On her introduction to my family, her first words were to tell my grandad that her grandfather also followed the Buddha. That made Grandad break into a giant smile. Anyway, anytime we went out together, everyone assumed she was 100% Nepalese.

For my wedding, we had two ceremonies. The first was the traditional package. The temple, the full set of rituals, a large hall and a big buffet feast. Mona's family had gone along. In fact, they *insisted* on the rituals. The next day, we had a Western-style reception. That was a black tie, sit-down dinner and an evening of pop entertainment. Two cousins and their families had flown in from Kathmandu. Mona and I were so nervous about being asked to dance in front of four hundred people. Grandad never looked happier. He spoke to every guest with an overflowing glass and kept on going to the kitchen to get hot *mōmō*, forcing them onto every person he met. For months after the wedding, he shared many anecdotes about the people he met. After a while, his stories also merged into his own wedding and that of my dad's.

The phone beeps again. At work, I would plan any difficult meetings in advance. Right now, I have no excuses. I have a tingling sensation in my mouth from the chilli in the pasta, and now sweat is building at the back of my neck. I find the comfiest spot on the large sofa in the living room.

Kaya's voice is sweet. The same as when she was a little girl. She starts with pleasantries and then adds, 'Uncle, how are things with the planning?'

I wish she would call me *māmā*, the proper Nepali word for uncle. I try to blag around the facts. Her voice becomes monotone, like Peter on a bad day.

She says, 'You promised to find the perfect venue; all we have is a long list. Your spreadsheet is wrong, it's a copy-and-paste from my cousin's wedding seven years ago. It's missing many relatives from my dad's side. And nothing has been done to book the officials.'

I am gripped by a hollowness in my chest. The back of my neck is wet. I remember this sensation when I missed two milestones in a work project two years ago. I had taken a blasting from Peter. 'Look, Kaya, give me a bit more time. I will work on the venue next week and come back to you. I have two or three places in mind already ...' My voice trails off. I search for something positive to add.

Her sweet voice splutters back. 'Speak next week, Uncle. Bye.'

The phone is dead before I can add anything. I throw the phone onto the sofa opposite and close my eyes. I can see Kaya – as a little girl with tears on her cheeks. And then I see a more haunting image: my grandad – his head bowed, almost falling over, his face on his hands, weighed down by loss of pride.

At 11 p.m. I am under the duvet, but I can't sleep. I go downstairs and check my phone. There is a text from Peter: 🚀 *I have informed your new team* 😃. *The company has great faith in you.* 💪

CHAPTER 2

TRAGEDY

The Friday after, I remember the missed call from Raff two days ago. I call him as soon as I am on the sofa at home. It's been four weeks since we played squash. I clench my teeth. It has always been me cancelling the game.

'Aman, I am going to give in my notice next week. I want to spend my time in a more meaningful way. I remember what you said last year about making bold decisions.'

I can't remember ever saying that. The sofa creaks as I shift. I hear myself sigh, 'Raff, this is ridiculous, you need to ride out this storm. You'll forever have politics in your life. How are you going to have a nice lifestyle with a pay cut this large? You want to work at a college but what about the politics and pressure there? I have heard it is endemic in education.'

Raff's voice is stronger: 'Listen, you may be right, but I will be doing things that matter – which is helping to educate young people with skills to be better citizens.' I hear a sharp intake of breath. I imagine Raff's plump hands gripping his mobile. 'Better still, I will educate myself. The college I have applied to has kids from all backgrounds. I want to know about other people's worlds, not become isolated in my own.'

I open and fold the magazine on the table next to me till there is a permanent crease. 'That's all well and good – but economies can't survive unless organisations sell products and services to each other. You are contributing by selling solar infrastructure – which is much better than selling digital art to affluent people.'

We go back and forth like a lengthy rally in squash. For every objection I raise, Raff has a counterargument. Fifteen minutes later, his belief remains unshaken. One thing I know about my best friend is that sometimes he won't budge. Yet, he agrees with my suggestion to conduct some further research.

***

On Monday at 7 p.m., I am a mile away from home. My headlights are on and there is a steady drizzle. I haven't seen any sun for a week. An alert pops up on my car dashboard to call Raff. I am hoping he has changed his mind, or at least that he waits a while. His phone rings twice, followed by a dead tone. Raff has never done that to me; if busy, he lets it go to voicemail. I call again and the same thing happens, but this time after a solitary ring. Surprised, I switch on the radio; Pearl Jam's 'Man of the Hour' is playing on Radio Two. I gifted Raff their greatest hits, re-released on vinyl two years ago. We used to listen to the band's album on a loop at university. Raff's favourite line from the song was: *Young men they pretend, old men comprehend.* The first thing Raff and I did after graduation was to see them perform at Reading Festival.

Fifty metres from the house, my car dashboard changes colour. The green telephone light is blinking. It's Sunita. She only ever calls me on my birthday. I automatically say, 'Is everything alright?'

'Raff's passed aw ...' is all she says before I can hear sobbing, her voice muffled like she has a hanky covering the phone.

I can't get any words out of my mouth. The car lights remain at full beam on my driveway. I shout, 'No, no.'

After that, I only remember her saying, 'A ... car crash with a lorry.'

My throat is dry. The bottom of my throat is having tiny muscle spasms.

Somehow, I make it into the kitchen. My phone is on loud-speaker. Sunita breathes out long and slow. I turn on the filter tap. The water makes a big ripple into the glass.

My hand is shaking without any command. Water is splashing onto my shirt and the floor. Sunita's voice is throbbing, and the way she is sobbing makes me think that water is going to come out of the speaker. She repeats twice, 'Raff and I were going to make a pie for dinner.'

My time with Raff at uni floods back.

I broke my leg at university, and he sacrificed a week of his studies to keep me company. I would never have met Mona without Raff. He had taken me to her at a mutual friend's party, with the strange line, 'Aman, this is Mona. You both like fitness stuff. And your grandparents are from the same part of the world.' Afterwards, I was happy and angry at him. Angry because he assumed I would like Mona because of our shared origins. Happy because my future wife and I connected without discussing our heritage.

There is water dripping from my cheeks into the glass. I wipe my eyes with the kitchen cloth.

Sunita's voice is wavering a little less. 'It's crazy, Aman, last week he was complaining about the lorries on that A road.' She must be aware of my tears. 'He thought so well of you. He used to say, "Aman is more than even a brother to me". He was so happy to hear about your every success.'

I can't remember the rest of our conversation, but I agree to meet her tomorrow and take calls from friends. The kitchen door opens. Nadia and Nabin's expressions are like when they were five.

They hug me, stand with me for a few seconds, and then disappear. Neither has seen me cry this long before; the last time was a few tears during a film.

I call Mona, mixing up facts, and ask her to pick up my mum on her way back.

Mona spends more time with Mum than I do. But today, I need Mum by my side. She asks no questions and prepares *ālū-kāulī tarkārī*, our family favourite, while I pour out my disbelief to Mona. Mum knew Raff well – he used to visit during university breaks. The number of calls grows from friends and Raff's extended family. By my fifth call, I know the script by heart. I repeat it again and again, but each time I bring out some new fact about Raff.

In between, a whole host of memories flood back of Raff. They are like flashes from adverts. Our teenage holiday at nineteen to Cyprus, the time we drove four hundred miles north on a whim to see the Forth Bridge. And the time we almost ended up in a police cell for urinating in the fountain outside the Rijks Art Museum. That was one hell of a stag do.

By far the strongest one, I had locked away for sixteen years. Raff and Sunita had come around to our house every day for ten days, with warm food and fresh flowers. That lifted us. Mona had miscarried a year into our marriage.

At 9.30 p.m., in amongst the jumble of messages, I get a text from Peter: *The Vietnam deal is almost through – my dinner meeting with them nailed it – value is likely to be around £230–270K* 💰💰. *Well done A – they loved our clear, succinct and benefit-driven proposal.* 👏

The numbers are meaningless to me. My dad's face flashes into my mind. It is the face he had when he bought his first Mercedes. He would have loved the '£' sign and the length of the number, but he is gone, and so is Raff.

I have no desire to sleep at all, so I slump on the sofa. Mona sits to my left, holding my hand under the blanket but says nothing. The flicker of the TV in the background has no audience.

At some point, I wake up in the living room all alone, with the side lamp still on and my head on my memory foam pillow from the bedroom. My heart has a piercing pain inside and my body has a four-beat throb. The TV is off. I stumble up the stairs, pillow in hand. The lounge clock says 3:20 a.m. There is not a sound from outside the house. But in my head is the sound of many drums beating.

Later that morning, I succumb to a headache. The pain is most intense on my forehead. My neck is completely stiff. I half open the curtains. Even with the tame winter light, I blink rapidly. The elderly neighbour from no. 21 is going out for his morning walk. His steps are slow and deliberate, like nothing matters. In the mirror, there are stripy red blotches on my face. The bedroom clock says 10:41 a.m. I send a text to the office and ignore the seventeen unread messages. My legs are like jelly, and I roll into the middle of the bed.

More past events with Raff flood back, a big jumble of different moments from the twenty odd years I have known him. Lekh was like a brother when I was growing up. Raff was more than a brother from my first year at university. I force myself up. I have to get control of the mass of voices in my head.

There is a note on the fridge: *I couldn't cancel work at short notice. There is a bowl of fruit in the fridge. Please have it. I don't think you should go to work. L U. I will try to get home early. M.*

I empty the dishwasher a utensil at a time. Onto one of the pans come three drops of water. I touch the tears on my cheeks. They are like a leaky tap. My tummy is so tight. There are two black grapes on top of the fruit bowl. I take one grape and force it into my gullet.

My throat throbs, and I want to throw up the grape. But it starts travelling down into my stomach. One part of me wants to go back to bed and the other part is desperate for company. There are twenty-one messages, every one about Raff. I read each syllable – it lessens my chest pain, but I don't reply to one. Afterwards, I stand in the shower until the water goes tepid.

***

The no. 71 sign is below the large blue knocker. He liked me to use that, even though he had a camera bell. The last time I stood here, it was Raff who opened the door. I move my hand to wave to the camera, hear the latch click and then see a bald and short version of Raff.

He holds his podgy hand out, 'Hi, I am Raff's brother.'

He doesn't bother asking me who I am. The door opens wider, and he steps back like I am someone important. Their kitchen is on the right, like ours, it's just smaller. Sunita is standing by the hob. Her face is glowing, but both eyes have small dark patches.

I give her a hug. Her body is warm, almost feverish. She half turns away and goes towards the worktop and then looks at the floor. A slow, steady stream of tears appears. She wipes them with her hand, but some make it to the grey tiles below. Her voice has a firmness.

'He was such a caring man. Throughout my illness, he hardly complained.'

Raff's brother is taking calls on top of the stairs; every word is clear. I want to burst into tears. I squeeze the top of the high stool by the large worktop. Sunita stares at my hand and pulls out three tomatoes from her fridge.

She says, 'Raff's brother is asking about the funeral process. I have never spoken to Raff about this. Have you?'

Raff came from parents of Indian heritage from Kerala. He was born in the Christian tradition, but Raff was an atheist. A Humanist, as he called himself at university.

Sunita doesn't wait for my answer. 'I am thinking of cremation – as soon as possible.'

That is what I was going to say. During a drunken chat after our final exams, before closing time in a pub, I had tried to convince Raff that cremation was always the better option. It was the fastest way of returning to mother nature. He had written an article in the university magazine on the ritual of death for his Humanist group.

Sunita takes a pan out and pours some water from the filter tap. She turns around and faces me for the first time. 'You look terrible, your face is scrunched up, Aman.' She hands me a knife and some washed salad. 'Help me with cutting.'

I dice the carrots. The knife is bulky but cuts without resistance. Two months ago, I told Raff that the Japan Shuna knife was thinner and had a superior cut, but he bought the sturdy German type.

'A few days ago, Raff told me, "Aman needs to get his priorities right. He dedicates himself to the technicalities at work but ignores other parts of his life."' Sunita empties the whole bag of penne into the water in the pan. 'He was happy you were also looking to make changes.'

She shakes her head. 'Raff had applied for a job at the college in Uxbridge and got an interview. He was so excited. But now he won't have a chance for this new chapter in his life.' She turns the knob on the gas hob. The blue light is shaking as it hits the pan bottom. She stands by the pan, peering into it.

I chop the pieces of carrot into tinier ones. I can hear Sunita's breath deepen. I turn around and see two tears roll from her face into the hot pan.

'Simi is coming back on a flight this evening.' Simi and Sunita used to have mother–daughter fights all the time, according to Raff. 'Our daughter was so nice on the phone. It felt like how things were two years ago.' She smiles for the first time since I arrived.

I arrange the tiny carrots on the chopping board, making the shape of a bangle. I want to take Raff's knife home as a memento.

An hour later, I piece together the facts from Raff's brother. My friend's car skidded and rolled over onto the road after hitting the pavement, and then into the side of an articulated lorry. His head took the brunt, and he didn't have a chance, even with the airbags deployed. They sent an air ambulance and spent an hour trying to revive him.

***

The next three days feel like a movie in fast forward. All my energy is spent just being around. The day before the funeral, we spend three hours going through photos and choosing fifteen to show at the crematorium. Sunita and Simi both turn to each other. The picture they share is of the three of them in a forest. The backdrop is dark green shrubs and the ultramarine blue sky. Tears roll out of their eyes in synchronicity.

The next day, the final rites take place. I am the coffin bearer and make a short speech about our friendship, but I can't remember any of the details. My brain is like glue, and I process things based on intuition and the prompts from the usher. Simi and Sunita are in the front seats holding hands. Just two of our mutual friends from university have turned up. They are sitting right at the back.

I cannot understand the process of mourning over a dead body. For me, the spirit or soul, if it existed, has already left. The body is nothing to mourn over – an empty vessel.

Raff lives in my mind and will forever be there. For the first time in years, I wish I had some alcohol inside me.

When I was fifteen, a parcel arrived with Nepalese stamps. My grandad had said, 'This is a handcrafted cup made from Kathmandu clay at my friend's factory. Back home, we drink alcohol in it, called *ai-lā*.'

My dad had rebelled against any organised religion and overextended my grandad's interest in alcohol. This ended up in cirrhosis of his liver at fifty-seven. The image of empty gin bottles from my childhood still sickens me.

At university, though, I discovered that alcohol was necessary for a social life. I had gone along with drinking rituals. In the final year of my degree, alcohol deadened the stress of taking exams. I want the feeling of emptiness to disappear right now.

One of our mutual friends is a rich pharmacist with a chain of sixteen shops. I hadn't spoken to him for two years, but we exchanged banter on our WhatsApp group. He finds me in the crematorium gardens. He has dark tracks under his eyes. His tummy is poking out of his T.M.Lewin shirt. I see his Porsche parked in the car park with the number plate 'MAX7'. In his hand, he has the biggest bouquet of flowers, each a different colour and shape. He grips my hand and doesn't let go for a few seconds. His Rolex watch is the starring role on his body, a Submariner with the royal blue facia. He promises to keep in touch but is the second to leave the gardens.

As the last few people leave, I arrange all the flower bouquets on the floor. The limousine goes with Raff's family and mine. A hand touches my shoulder. I turn around, one knee off the floor, and lose balance. The same hand stops me from falling over. I look up. It's Lekh, looking the same as he did when I last saw him three years ago. That was at a wedding where we had ignored each other, and I only exchanged a superficial chat with his wife and kids. What the hell is he doing here? In a flash, memories of Lekh, Raff and I playing pool during university summer breaks flood my mind.

I stand up and straighten my tie.

Lekh says, 'Alright?' in the soft voice that Grandad loved. He looks in my eyes. 'Can I have a lift back with you to Sunita's house? I came on the tube.'

I fold my arms. I can hardly say no. In the car, he says nothing for the first five minutes. The first traffic light is a busy junction with five roads. Lekh is looking at the people crossing. His shirt is a standard blue. I bet it's M&S. I stare at the red light. It feels like it will stay that colour forever.

Lekh says, 'Do you think Raff died happy?'

'I guess so. He was about to embark on a fresh career, and his mind was free. And you heard an hour ago how he loved the volunteer work on Saturday mornings teaching Maths. A sign of a man at peace with himself.'

Lekh keeps looking at the pedestrians. 'And how do you feel?'

My stomach turns hot like the warmth of the red light. The pedestrians stop crossing. I hit the accelerator. Once on the other side, I lose control of my words. 'My whole life, I have not once thought properly about death until now. I mean, I spoke to Raff last week ... and now he's gone.'

Out of the corner of my eyes, I can see him blinking like a butterfly. He hasn't lost that trait from childhood. It means he is thinking. 'I am glad that Raff got cremated. More and more people are doing it. Do you know why Buddhists prefer cremation?'

He doesn't wait for me to answer. 'The physical body has no significance to our faith; it's a vessel for holding our soul.' He looks at me. 'I like how the chaplain conducted the ceremony, a celebration of Raff's contribution towards others.'

My body is a vessel for throbbing pain. My mum used to repeat a phrase anytime Lekh came up in a conversation. I can hear her saying it now. 'Lekh is so thoughtful and balanced, with a voice that matches.' Anytime she praised Lekh, my face used to go warm.

I wish I had never given him a lift.

Two days later, I am back in the office. It's also the day I move up one floor.

***

Someone has moved my small cupboard, 34-inch screen and decorated mugs. My desk has the best natural light near the long window. The view from the fourth floor is an upgrade alright. At last, I can make out St Paul's Cathedral in its full glory and there are more jet streams in the sky. And then I look up at the drop ceiling; right above me is where all the directors sit. If my dad were around, he would be on the phone, calling up all our cousins on the pretext of catching up, but then go straight into talking about my promotion.

George arrives an hour later with an army rucksack and rumbles around his desk cupboard. I am perplexed about why Peter has asked George to join my team. Most days, I see George wandering around and socialising. He reminds me of the types I have met in my career, people who coast and contribute nothing but talk endlessly. Ten minutes later, he sits down in the chair opposite and stretches his legs. 'Was it a relative or a mate?'

He wants me to blab everything out. I turn my head back to my screen. After my dad died, I went into overdrive with my work, burning up as many hours as I could. It had helped me at the time. An hour later, I am in Peter's office. 'Aman, we had a massive issue yesterday with delivering those images due to the server load. That customer in Taiwan is a little pissed off, to say the least.'

It is my first time hearing Peter use the 'p' word. I wish I was in bed.

He continues, 'I know you were at a funeral, but now you are back …'

My mouth is bitter, and I am grinding my teeth. My heart feels like it is going to sink into my stomach. Peter didn't even ask me how I feel.

On the lift down, I am alone at last. I close my eyes.

I imagine slamming my fist into the lift wall. 'I am only a number,' I say out loud. But for this place, it may be an important one. Peter is right. All I need to do is think about work.

***

Five weeks later, we meet up with our biggest potential client, ArtCloudo. Peter has got the CEO's PA to book a swanky meeting room overlooking Trafalgar Square, in sight of the National Gallery.

With me is Louis, one of my juniors, an American whose accent is a strange mixture of 'home counties English' and Texan, which amuses me. Three months ago, he earned a lot of kudos after resolving a database issue involving corruption in our digital art asset prices – an issue that, in his words, saved us 'a few bucks.' Louis's pecs make him look like he is an Adonis from the gym, but what sticks out is his nose. It reminds me of the artist Ghirlandaio's portrait of *An Old Man and his Grandson*. The Renaissance painting has an extraordinary feature – a deformity of the old man's nose. Apparently, some disease. The child in the painting has a delicate, kind face, not bothered about the older man's looks.

Louis has an interesting backstory. I heard through the office grapevine that he found himself homeless after buying a one-way ticket to London, and that he knew no-one when he arrived.

He finally got placed into DigiArt via a charity. His potato-shaped nose and his deep-set eyes hint at his difficult background. Today, Louis has the mesmerising look of the child in the painting, after all, this is the first time he is at a sales meeting.

Peter's tie is a new one, flowery green with a silky look. No-one wore ties last year; now it's the new fashion. The analogue clock is at ten to eleven.

I fidget and look down at my Notes app.

Peter strokes his tie, then says, 'This would be a brilliant start to this revenue stream if we win this work. Funnily enough, Joan and I used to go to the same fencing club in the late 90s. I never imagined she'd end up so high, but, hey, times have changed.'

ArtCloudo has been in continuous touch over the last ten days, and we are on the cusp of agreeing a contract. Four days ago, I put the final proposal through to their director Joan Preston with three options for implementation.

Joan arrives with an entourage of two. The large hand of the clock is nearing the ten-minute mark. There is no apology. They settle with expertise around the table. The three of them are equidistant apart, opposite Peter and me. Louis parks himself at the very end where the table turns oval.

Joan looks at Peter. 'Well, it's been so many years since I gave you a salute at the foil.' She bends her back for a moment. 'I hope your family is well.'

Peter gives a nondescript response. I never realised the two of them had history.

Joan opens her device and scrolls down. 'Well, Peter, you have done so well in the business world, I tracked your achievements on LinkedIn. I thought you were not much of an art fan,' she says, glancing at my right shoulder.

Peter is hardly ever on the back foot. As he stirs the tea in the porcelain teapot he replies, 'Art nowadays is interesting.' His face is no longer jutting. He hands over a full cup and the plate of Bourbon biscuits to Joan.

I pull up the proposal on the 50-inch LCD screen and explain our method for delivery. Joan taps her device on the table and looks straight at me, ignoring the screen. I want to get to the end of my carefully prepared presentation. Instead, I sit down in the nearest chair. The presentation is on the finance slide. She thrusts herself forward and her gaze moves between Peter and me.

She says, 'Let's get to the finer details of scope. A pay-per-use model, rolling contract for six months. Limited to your sixteenth- and seventeenth-century range of art, including Asia.'

Peter has a half smile. His eyes look bluer. This is exactly the option we wanted. He moves his slim body an inch forward. But his hands are still folded. Maybe her direct stare is something he encountered during fencing.

The dull chimes of Big Ben resonate from my left. We booked the meeting room for two hours but finish thirty minutes early. This is by far the largest contract I've ever won.

As soon as we hear the whirr of the lift taking Joan down, Peter breaks into the widest smile I have ever seen. 'Aman, this is fabulous! This is a great start for you and the team.'

I want him to take me to lunch at The Ochre atop the National Gallery.

'But there is no time to celebrate today. Initiate the work with our technical partners on the second floor so we don't get caught short.'

I stay behind to fire off some emails. On my way to the station, my legs falter as I walk past the National Gallery.

The digital advert says, *Terrific Titian – only two weeks left.* I haven't seen many of Titian's paintings. It says the collection contains loans from galleries in Venice and Florence. That slow deep pleasure of seeing great paintings may be better than the fleeting high of winning a big contract. Who knows when there will be such a display again. I want to turn towards the queue, but my steps quicken.

That afternoon, Louis comes to my desk as I am about to leave. 'Boss, I solved it! Remember the data duplication issue we had? I have figured it out – it's our input code and referencing error that added false data.'

I stand up and give him a fist bump. I love being called 'Boss'; it's one of the few American slang terms I like.

***

At the end of December, our business-class flight lands in Dubai. Mona had asked me if we should cancel it in light of Raff's death.

I'd said, 'That makes no sense. We need to push ahead and not let this get us down. Raff would have wanted me – us – to take this holiday.'

The whole holiday is loaded on my credit card. 22k is the most I have paid for an exotic trip.

When we arrive, I don't bother going to our room. Instead, I whizz around, snapping photos inside the building, onto the beach and inside again. I check off everything I have seen on the Instagram page of the hotel. The pictures are sent to my contacts – basically, anyone I interacted with in the last two weeks. Kaya is the first to reply. If Raff was alive, he would have commented on my snaps with some cryptic reply.

Our hotel stands on an artificial island. The whole place is like a well-orchestrated painting. No aspect is overlooked. At its centre is a mock Hindu temple with accommodation blocks enveloped in its light. It's as if a whole street has been transported from the East.

Every lift assistant calls me by my name. For the next week, I hear 'Good morning' or 'Good day, Mr Pradhan' over and over again. I never tire of those words.

Every morning after breakfast, the kids disappear. They never have dinner with us – feasting out on junk food at the earlier seating at 6 p.m. Yesterday evening before bedtime, Nabin and Nadia told us of two giant water slides, a huge trampoline and the 24/7 snack bar. Mona spends most of the time on the beach, reading a book. I roam around the hotel, taking photos of its décor. Instagram is my partner.

On the third day, the evening entertainment has a Queen theme. Mona and I are sitting a few metres from the stage. Her cheeks are shining. She reaches out and holds my hand. The band plays 'The

Show Must Go On'. That song was my dad's favourite. It was also one of the few songs Raff liked from the 80s. I know every word.

Mona pulls her hand away and touches my face. There are tears dripping onto the napkin. I brush her hand off and pretend to blow my nose. I look left and right. No-one else has noticed.

'Shall we go to the lounge and talk or back to our room?' she says.

My eyes feel hot. I reply in her ear, 'No, it's okay; I have no idea where that came from.'

I catch up with the singer's words and start humming.

Three days into the holiday, I put my camera away. My laptop is open, and the base is too warm to touch. Mona is under the umbrella on the beach, and the kids are on the water slides. Punching the keyboard and answering emails is my comfort zone. My window has a view onto a palm tree and part of the beach.

There is a knock at the door. The staff member who enters can't be more than twenty-one. He looks like he is from the subcontinent. I stay in the room. He starts making the bed.

I say, without reducing my typing rate, 'You been working here long?'

He is removing every crease from the pillow before putting it carefully back in place.

He doesn't look at me as he says, 'Four years.'

I stop typing and say, 'Are you alone?'

His voice is now more natural. 'Yes, sir. My family is back home in India.'

I say, 'Oh, I hope you see them soon.'

I look at the immaculate wallpapered ceiling. He moves back towards the bathroom entrance.

'Mr Pradhan, I haven't been home for two years. Sir, there are no paid holidays.' He hesitates and then continues, 'Pay is 800 dirhams a month. Half goes back to my village near Patna, and the rest is rent. But I get free food, as much as I want. Do you want extra bottles of water?'

I hold out the empty bottle at my desk.

He comes forward. 'I will leave a large sparkling one for you, Mr Pradhan.'

I close my laptop lid and give him a thumbs up. He blinks at my left hand and eyes my watch.

His voice is excited, and he shows all his teeth and a dimple. 'One day, I will buy my dad a Rolex.'

I drop my left hand and scratch my leg even though there is no itch. I lift my laptop lid as high as possible. I fix my gaze on the first open email I can find. Out of the corner of my right eye, I see his face. His dimple has disappeared.

The latched door shuts before I can respond. I wish I hadn't spoken to him. I make a vow to avoid talking to anyone from the subcontinent at the resort.

On the last day, a person in a suit with the hotel emblem finds Mona and me sitting at the outdoor café. It's 28°C, and he hasn't got a bead of sweat on his forehead.

'Mr and Mrs Pradhan, would you like to eat in the 7-star Indian restaurant this evening? We have a tasting menu for just 300 dirhams. Your kids can be looked after at the grand buffet.'

'Per person?' I ask.

He gives a single slow nod as if I am a child.

I raise my eyebrows and look at Mona. She shuts her book, using the menu as a bookmark.

She waits till the suit has gone. 'That's an exorbitant price, even here.' She sits up straighter. 'I spoke to the beach guard today. He is from Western Nepal – a place furthest away from Kathmandu. He works six days a week, you know, and lives thirty miles away from here in a place called Ajman. Gets bussed in. Works twelve-hour shifts. Earns 800 dirhams a month. That's £200 – and most of his cash goes back home.' When Mona speaks, as if she is making a list, it tells me she is upset. Mona's eyes are dark even with the bright lights of the café. 'Has a 5-foot single bed in a shared flat with six others. How can you live like that?'

'They have a job; that's the important thing. Anyway, life here is miles better than in the East. Our money is going to help them.'

Mona shakes her head and puts her hands on her eyes. 'But they are far away from family. Plus, they have no security.' She looks at the plane climbing in the sky. 'You could be on the journey to Dubai from Nepal if your grandad hadn't got immigration rights to the UK.' The plane pans past us. It's an Airbus double-decker. From the emblem, I know the top deck is all business class.

I say, 'Grandad has always said that rich or poor is all part of karma. Cause and effect of good or bad deeds. But if Dad was here he would agree with me – my hard work has brought me to this wonderful place, nothing else.'

She shakes her head, this time with more vigour. Her thumb finds the bookmark.

My grandad and dad, however, used to get into feuds that I could never make sense of. Grandad always used to be so proud of Dad in public. But every few months, they used to have heated arguments, either about Dad drinking or his attachment to money. It was always in Nepalbhasa, so I only got fragments of it. Afterwards, they both pretended nothing happened.

On the flight back, we are on the top deck. I am next to a man about ten years older than me. Apart from my neighbour and me, everyone else's seats are fully flat with blankets on.

My film ends and I take my headphones off and stretch. I glance at my neighbour; he has the same Rolex watch as me, the Daytona, just one design up. He turns his head round and looks at the bracelet on my right hand.

'So, what business do you own?'

One piece of advice my grandad gave me was never to lie, but he also told me you don't have to always tell the truth. 'I am a leader of a business that specialises in art digitisation.'

'Wow, you are one of those start-ups. You must be swimming in investment money from Dubai. Me, I was lucky. My dad passed his engineering business to me, and I have run it ever since.' He looks out of the window at the bright lights of some city.

'Isn't Dubai perfect in the UK winter? I started flying upper deck – well, my son insisted I should. Now I love it. No other way to travel.' He chuckles, lifting his hand near the brim of the wine glass. He looks to the floor. 'The thought of going economy is frightening.'

I put my headphones back on and search for my next film. Good job he doesn't know of my Amex bill.

***

Mona asked me yesterday in bed, after the lights were out, if I wanted to talk about Raff. I refused. Getting through each day is my sole goal. I ignore all the voices that come every day. Sometimes it's my grandad, sometimes my dad, once it was Lekh, but most of the time, it's Raff.

Once at a sermon at the *Bāhā*, the visiting monk had said, 'The Buddha said to live in every moment, not to spend time on the past.' That's what I am trying to do. But the voices keep coming, the sound is endless. My mind says at some point, they must go away; infinite is just a mathematical term.

***

A month later, I have a voicemail from Kaya. I have managed to keep her off my back since returning from Dubai. I sent her the list of invitations, being careful not to miss out distant cousins and family friends.

This wedding, like mine, is a big occasion for our family. But the venue, décor and theme are all yet to be decided. One part of me wants to abandon this project and hand it back to my sister, but the other part is where my conscience bites.

Grandad explained my role at Kaya's naming ceremony. He said, 'To be a *māmā* is something to take great pride in. You will understand as Kaya grows.' Grandad was right. I taught Kaya to walk when she was with us one weekend at eleven months old. I took her to primary school on her first day, as my sister had hurt her ankle playing tennis. Now that my sister and her husband are far away in Mauritius, Mona says I am a combination of both big brother and surrogate dad.

As I walk to the door of my house, I see two empty drinks cans in my front garden. I shake my head, turning and staring at my neighbour's house. They have an old-fashioned red door knocker, and I want to tap it hard.

I reach out with my electronic key at the front door. I can hear Nadia's distinct voice behind our thick UPVC door: 'Dad never seems to be sorting things out. Kaya's still so worried about the wedding. Our tech issue hasn't been fixed. For God's sake, he's supposed to be the expert at solving problems. The power sockets in my room don't work. How am I supposed to charge my phone and use my hairdryer?'

I want to drive around the block for another ten minutes. The talking inside continues. I put my key back in my pocket and wave my hand by the camera doorbell.

Nadia opens the door. 'Hi Dad, is the encryption on the key broken?' She emphasises *encryption* like she is trying to impress me. She flashes a wry smile, turns and retreats to the living room.

I head straight upstairs, not bothering to take off my shoes. I want to lie down. The ladder at the top of the stairs is extended from the ceiling. I look up through the orange tinge of the loft light on the ladder. Nabin's feet are visible near the hatch.

'What are you doing up there, Nabin?' I shout.

'Well Dad, the TV picture is awful, as you know,' he says in a grown-up tone. 'I thought I'd come and fix it myself. I saw a YouTube video that said sometimes rust builds on the digital connection, or there is something—'

I cut Nabin off mid-sentence. 'It's dangerous there. You could get electrocuted. Come down. I will find some repair guy to try and sort this.'

Nabin replies with a groan, 'But Dad, I can fix it, you keep telling me to get to the root cause and that's what I am doing. The video by RepairJo taught me where to look on the amplifier box. There may be two causes, not just one, Dad, according to RepairJo. Please let me have a go!'

There is a sinking sense in my stomach. Nabin's thinking is sound, but I have no mental energy left to fix this problem.

'Come down now. Let me get an expert in, you shouldn't be playing with electrical connections.'

Nabin jumps off the second to last rung. His ears are crimson. He looks away from my gaze. His lips are locked as if sealed by glue. He marches to his room and slams the door shut. I imagine him behind the door with his thumbs on his Xbox, attacking some monsters as vengeance.

My head throbs. I want to run out of the house. My face feels hot. If only my team could see my management skills now. I turn to my phone and ask the AI to find a telecoms repairer. I pick the one with 5-star reviews. My haste will probably mean someone expensive.

The repair man arrives three days later in a lovely, branded van. The man has smart ultramarine-coloured overalls. He hardly talks. Not like our builder. Nabin tags along with him, as if connected by a short rope. After some clicks and bumps that echo in the loft, he comes down the ladder and stands at its foot. Nabin remains in the loft.

'One of the connections had rust, so I just cleaned it and opened the chip amplifier to have a peek inside. It's only two years old, but full of dust inside, which makes it intermittent. I have a spare in the van. Best you change it over to avoid another job in a few months.'

He looks at me, 'I can see why you haven't gone for getting all your content via the new stream box. You can't trust technology, can you?' He nods his head and laughs. 'And I agree, who knows who is watching us?'

The bill comes to £170 for about ninety minutes of work. The man taps my credit card on his device, taking my money in under thirty seconds.

Within minutes of him leaving, I search for *digibox amplifier* on the web. A nice cobalt-coloured one comes up for £19.

Nabin is hovering right near me and says, 'See Dad, I told you RepairJo was right on YouTube. It was the power amplifier and the connection. We could have done it ourselves. The repair guy said I was right and that I would make a great engineer.'

For £170, I can get a miniature replica of a Renaissance painting for the bathroom, perhaps something by Titian.

Nabin gazes into my eyes.

I force out the words, 'Well done Nabin, yes, you were right.' I gaze at his shining right ear and avoid his eyes.

Back in my room, I jump on the bed. I skim through some of Titian's two hundred and fifty paintings on my iPad. Many of them use an ultramarine blue to depict the sky and clothing. The colour itself signalled status for it was a rare paint, made using a precious stone from Asia. Grandad had told me that it was still mined in Nepal.

After dinner, I hand the last bowl to Mona as she loads the dishwasher. She turns around.

'Can we talk for a few minutes?'

The kids empty the kitchen at speed. I wipe the table clean, wash my hands and place myself on the seat furthest away from Mona. She adds a tablet and presses the start button.

I press the sleep button on my phone. A picture of Raff and his family is up as the phone wallpaper.

Sunita, from what I know from Mona, is coping as well as can be. She has returned to work and her health is good. I ring her every now and then, but Mona calls her more. She seems to be coping with Raff's loss better than me. Raff always said she was the most grounded person he ever met. I must visit her, but the thought of using the blue door knocker at no. 71 petrifies me. It will increase the flood of memories for me to drown in.

Mona removes a magnet from a piece of paper attached to the fridge and then sits opposite me. The dishwasher hum gets louder.

'I wanted to wait a little while to give you time to grieve over Raff's going. But we need to get a few things sorted at home.' She puts the paper between us and turns it so I can't miss what's on it. 'Here is a list of things that need fixing. We agreed you would do all the repairs. I just don't have the time to do them unless you want to start doing more of the cooking?'

Her eyelashes are spread wide. I pull the paper towards me. It lists about a dozen things, all in joined-up writing. It includes the broken pressure cooker hood, new blinds, broken sockets, the leak in the garage roof, lock fittings on the windows, an ivy infestation in the garden, the TV picture (crossed off), and a broken roof tile.

She puts her arm on my left shoulder. I let it stay. My legs are shaking under the table.

'Can you get the builder to come?'

I clench my toes hard. I grab the list. Most of the small jobs I can do myself. I want to scrunch up the list and drown it inside the dishwasher.

Our builder left school at sixteen and did an apprenticeship. He is honest but takes more time than needed on the job. When we first met, I told him I studied telecoms engineering at university and was 2% from getting a first class. I wanted him to acknowledge my grades, but he'd gone back to turning his ratchet screwdriver.

Three months ago, I called him to change the flush mechanism on the toilet. It was a simple lift and replace and it took about three minutes to do the work. Plus, another twenty minutes of chat as he explained the details of the bathroom refit that he was doing for someone else.

He needs to do some real work, which is to build me a loft conversion and fit out a games room. Now, I am thinking a pool table rather than ping-pong. I estimate the cost is going to be £50,000, maybe £60,000. Even with my pay rise, it will need an extension of my twenty-year mortgage, but that should be easy to get from the bank and anyway, it will raise the value of our home.

Mona takes her arm off my shoulder.

I say, 'But these jobs are easy, I just have to find the time. You know the pressure I am under at work.'

Mona's cheeks are flushed. This phenomenon is infrequent, but I know what it means. She is going to go through all the areas where I mess up. One by one. With no holding back.

My phone is facing her. She sees the picture of Raff and his family on the screen. She sighs out loud. Then there is silence. She pats my shoulder and shuts the kitchen door behind her. I want to open the dishwasher and throw the list in, but instead put it back on the fridge.

Since Dubai, every evening, I sit here with my headphones, listening to music I loved from the start of the new century. That's when Raff and I were at university. At the same time, I browse through social media and eat whatever sweet snacks I can find. I haven't joined the family in the living room since Raff died. Nobody in this home seems to realise how garbled my mind is. Mona's threat worries me. More cooking would be a chore, but it's worse than that – I know my wife is quite good at fixing things. Our honeymoon was at a villa in Antalya. I broke a wardrobe by putting our heavy suitcase on it. I freaked out as, according to the owner, it was an expensive antique Ottoman piece. Mona had it all fixed by the time I returned from my errand to the deli a mile away.

Louis and I have fixed three complex issues on the ArtCloudo database this week and Louis looks up to me for my mentoring skills. Now, I can't even conjure up a plan to fix simple things in the house.

***

About a fortnight later, on my way to work, Kaya calls.

'Are you on your hands-free, Kaya? You shouldn't talk when driving.'

I shouldn't have asked, as the sound of keyboard clicking tells me she is already at her office. I tell Kaya the work I have done on the invitation list and the shortlist of venues.

'Uncle, I am convinced the Rayish venue is the place. I went there yesterday evening. You will love the paintings on their walls. Apparently, they are replicas of famous frescoes. The place is so elegant. But the cost is so exorbitant, I can't afford £4,000 for the day and don't want to ask Mum and Dad for more money. We need to look for something else, but we need to do this quickly.' Her voice is not as sweet as normal.

I want to tell Kaya I will take on the cost for the venue. It's something Grandad would have applauded. Instead, I say, 'Look, Kaya, let me speak to them and negotiate. You are right, the price is a bit high. Give me a few days to visit their manager.'

Kaya's voice gets louder and quicker as she goes through her list of what's remaining for planning. My chest feels like there are some dumbbells on it. Finding the venue is just the start for the wedding.

CHAPTER 3

THE RISE

———————————————

Today holds the possibility of signing our second-largest deal. So far, we have won twelve smaller deals and one very big one. An excited buzz runs through our team as we finalise the proposal. Opposite me are Emily, Louis and two other juniors. Emily is the only person who has come from my old team on the third floor. I jerk my shoulder as someone taps it hard. I look up. George is grinning.

He laughs and says, 'Sorry, didn't mean to frighten you. You ready for the meet?'

There is sweat on the top of my lip.

Behind closed doors, I ask him, 'Do you have any concerns, George, is anything bothering you? Do you need any support with the reporting processes?'

His feet are tapping under the table. He yawns once. I want to ask him if he is up to the job. But everything he has done in the last few days has been acceptable. I have nothing to pick him up on.

He says, 'All is good. Ta.' He stares at the clock behind me.

When I imagine my team's future, I don't see George in it. I have to find a way to get rid of him.

Ten minutes later, I open the door and find Peter waiting outside. He is wearing his blue and green tie, which means he is in a good mood. George laughs as Peter makes a joke about some serial on Netflix last night. Their casual chat annoys me. He taps his knuckles at the electronic whiteboard, displaying my grid with the title *winning new clients* and puts his right thumb up.

He says, 'I was passing by and thought I'd say hello. Well done, Aman, to you and the *team*. I can see a lot of movement since we started this new function.'

He certainly wasn't passing by; he was checking up on me. I wonder why he emphasises the word *team*.

I stand up to get closer to his height. He holds the door handle, hesitates and then releases it. He sits on the edge of the table and gestures to me. My backside hits the chair, jolting it. I want to bite my nails.

He says, 'As you know, a new director's role will open up later this year. You should consider it ...' His phone pings. He waves his hand and heads to the lift without a second look.

I stand up. My head is light. I sit back down involuntarily. Could this be the opportunity I have been waiting for? Was Peter hinting at me? He must be, otherwise why mention it?

My legs start vibrating. I have an urge to use up the energy welling up inside me. I am outside the building in a flash. Birds are singing as if it's the start of spring, but my mind is chirping with possibilities. I start walking east towards the sun as fast as I can. Ten minutes later, I see a large green space. I have never seen this park before and find the nearest empty bench. The same repeated thoughts are whirring around like the tyres of an F1 car. There is a sweet scent of flowers as the wind brushes past my face ... I stare at the tarmac path. There will definitely be a selection process for this role. My elation starts to seep away. I start tapping my heel into the ground. What if an outsider does well in the interview? I may get overlooked. What if Peter is toying with me as motivation for more effort? My hands are over my eyes.

'Are you alright?' says a new voice.

I look up. I can see pigeons about ten metres away pecking at the grass. I realise where I am. An old lady is sitting on the opposite side of the bench to me. She has grey hair and is wearing a heavy black coat. Her brown walking stick rests between us. She has a few more wrinkles than my mum. Her back stoops a little, but her face is alert, and her blue eyes have an attentive gaze.

I say nothing.

She continues, 'Whatever it is, it can't be so bad. You are so young. I am sure you will sort it out. Ups and downs of life never go away, you know.'

I want to burst out laughing. I keep my lips tight.

She points to the front. 'Look at those pigeons over there, they keep coming back. If there is no food one day, there will be some the next.'

The pigeons move en masse to the climbing frames twenty metres away.

She continues, 'They don't seem to get caught up in their own world.'

I want to tell her that her imagination is running wild. Instead, I nod at her twice like I did to my grandad. She gets up, using the full brunt of her stick. But at a quicker pace than my mum.

She says, 'Never mind about my blabbering. I must get going.'

Her back is already turned away from me before I can respond. I wait till she is out of earshot. Then I laugh out loud. The pigeons scurry away.

That afternoon, Emily and I are both brewing a drink in the kitchenette. I explain Kaya's forthcoming wedding and my significant role.

She says, 'Wedding planners can make such a difference. That's what we had for my nephew's wedding. It took the stress out of the arrangements. I am told they are brilliant at negotiating rates from venues. Planning at work is okay, but so different to a wedding. More complicated, don't you agree, Aman? And what about the families to manage? They are the most complex stakeholders. You mentioned that you have a large extended family. All part of your Asian heritage, right? You have a tradition of keeping in touch, right?'

The wedding planner details arrive via Emily later that afternoon. I call them at 6 p.m. on my way home. I get a recorded message with a professional voice. I leave a long message.

Grandad would disapprove.

***

On most Saturdays I take Nabin to his football game. That means I can stay in bed until 9:30 a.m. and then make the largest mug of tea with cinnamon on top. That's not all. I usually browse through some Renaissance paintings on my device over breakfast. Since I joined DigiArt, it has rekindled my interest in art. This time, I pick the frescoes of Ghirlandaio on the church walls in Florence.

The ping from my phone breaks my concentration. We had a planned early morning electricity outage for Saturday at the office. I am suspicious about Cloud security, even though all the experts say otherwise. Raff always told me never to take technical experts' words for granted. The fridge door opens. Nadia has crept in to get some fruit yoghurt. She slams the door, and the repair list falls from its magnet. She picks it up and puts it beside me. I feel a surge of heat in my heart. I put the list back on the fridge but upside down.

Nabin's football ground is a two-mile journey, but it still takes twenty minutes. At three junctions, I see cars passing by with children in the back seat. All have coloured tops on. My heart carries the guilt that I didn't take Nabin last week, but the proposal for the Indonesian customer was due.

Nabin says, 'It's going to be a tough game. Apparently, their defence is solid. But their main striker is injured.'

I love this banter with Nabin.

He continues. 'I have a feeling I will be playing in left-back today. Been told at the coaching last week to run down the wing more.'

I nod in agreement. I try my best to take an interest in football and like the competitive side. Growing up, I had two left feet and was always the last to be picked on the playground, which made my interest somewhat superficial.

'Uncle Kishan mentioned last week in the car that I would be better there than left-mid.'

Kishan is not my brother; he is my backup when I can't take Nabin. I had insisted to Nabin and Nadia that all adults are uncles or aunties. Grandad told me that's what everyone in Nepal did.

Nabin says at the second traffic light, 'Dad, my football bag's broken. You still need to fix it. The strap snapped off completely. It's hard for me to carry and feels even heavier.'

The bag is from an expensive brand, Tatonka. It's the same brand I used when I went on my one-and-only trek with Raff and his friends in my twenties. I sit in the car while Nabin and his teammates warm up. On Amazon, I find a bag in crimson on offer for 20% off the normal £44.95. I press the 'buy' button. That releases heat in my heart.

Kishan is already there when I get to the touchline. Always early. He makes a beeline towards me. Kishan never misses a Saturday, whether it's training or a match. His daughter is one of two girls in the football team. Unlike him, I always drift in and out of watching every kick. I use my time to plan domestic errands, make phone calls, or think through a work obstacle. Sometimes, I sit in my car and afterwards make some excuse to Nabin about my disappearance. But Kishan is always by the touchline, moving up and down with the flow of the game.

'Aman, how are you, mate? You missed a great game last week. The 1–1 does not give credit to the intensity,' he says with his bright eyes and open stance. Kishan wears the same checkered shirt and red sweater every week. He is portly, but his tummy is not prominent, and his shoulders are broad and strong. He looks like one of those cowboys in a Western.

His place of work, by his own description, is 'a posh oldies' home.' Kishan doesn't match my stereotype of a carer. He has a way with words and has the confidence of a lion. I see the same traits in his daughter. She goes for tackles with her whole heart and is not afraid to take charge when the situation demands it. A couple of boys, but not Nabin, are scared of her. I wonder why Kishan ended up working in a care home. He had not studied past his BTEC. Yet, everyone follows his lead when he puts down the nets at the end of a game.

He laughed when I offered him an interview as a supervisor in our contact centre last year. 'Man, an office job would wrench out my soul. You seem to think I don't like what I do. They pay me well, I get endless presents from our oldies' posh relatives and, what's more, I don't need to use a spreadsheet! Why give up my contentment?'

Fifteen minutes into the game, he says, 'You won't believe which old celebrity is in our care home at the moment ...' He stops mid-sentence. The referee has blown his whistle. An opposition player is on the floor grasping his ankle. Kishan wanders away.

I see him poking around his daughter's bag and he returns with something in hand.

'I see that Nabin's bag strap broke last week. It's easy to fix with this replacement – you need to remove the handles and buckle and fit it in again. If you want to strengthen it a bit, you can sew the top as well.' He pushes it into my hand.

This is exactly how Louis had approached and solved a problem when the software on our server farm wasn't working. After a bit of searching, he found some code that patched the server settings. In the end, it saved us buying an expensive piece of new software, with add-ons we didn't need. Why didn't I think of this solution?

It's 0–0 at halftime. I want to cancel my Amazon order and reach into my pocket. But Kishan won't stop talking. I am half-listening while worrying about the status of the office outage.

The whistle blows for the restart.

'My daughter wants to do software development if a football career doesn't work. Would you say that's a nice job? Does it pay well at all? What about the work hours?'

We both track his daughter, who blocks the opposition's lone striker and guides the football into touch.

I say, 'I am impressed she is already thinking of this. It's the right career. Process automation, AI and Cloud coding are all going to need deep software skills. Skills as important as Maths and English. Actually, did you know AI prediction algorithms support problem solving?'

I see Kishan's eyes open wide. I wish I hadn't been so technical. 'I tell you what, Kishan, send her around to my office during summer for a few days. I am sure she can learn a few things.'

The game ends in a draw. According to Kishan, neither team had the power in midfield to push forward.

I say to Nabin in the car, 'Kishan says you had a quiet game but put in some great tackles. I rate your performance seven out of ten. What do you think?'

Nabin used to love ratings when he started playing at seven. He doesn't reply. Instead, he twists the bag strap from Kishan.

Four days later, at 8 p.m., the courier knocks and the crimson Tatonka bag arrives on my doorstep. I yell 'Damn' as I shut the door. How did I forget to cancel the order? I go upstairs and show the bag to Nabin.

'Dad, I've already fixed the old bag with the strap from Uncle Kishan and the needle and thread Mum gave me. I don't want the new one. I prefer the old one as I am used to it.' He hands over the bag and says, 'You shouldn't waste hard-earned money.'

I burst out laughing. 'That's just what your great grandad would have said and all in Nepalbhasa.'

He shrugs his shoulders and forces his lips wide.

'I thought you would be excited to get this bag.'

I turn it around, so he has a better view. It has two deep side pockets for water and more padded back support. He shrugs again, twisting his neck like a shrug has its own language.

I mentally add 'return the bag' to my ever-growing list of things to do. The bag goes into the kitchen larder next to the sack of basmati rice.

The Monday after, I have a video meeting with a wedding planner at 5 p.m. A confident professional voice says, 'Our services use our bespoke planning software. We have a dedicated team, which will look after different tasks and use a planning matrix with you in mind. We provide a full range of extras, including flower arrangement, décor, and music.'

This sounds like one of the pitches I make with a client. I tap my feet as I wait for her to get to the end. That is when the price will be revealed. Fifteen minutes later, she says, 'For your type of wedding, our value-adding service is a very competitive £3,300.'

I press the red button. My brain hurts. The lady's tone sounds too much like mine. There is nothing she is offering that I couldn't do on my own. Okay, I can find the cash with my raise. But the blow to my ego would be hard to bear. This project is simple. At my wedding, Grandad insisted on getting the whole family to chip in. He used to sit by our landline phone, passing messages and easing conflict. I tap my heel into the floor. I am determined not to outsource Kaya's wedding.

***

A month later, on a Thursday afternoon, I am pounding the keyboard to get another proposal out when I notice a soft hand on my shoulder. I turn around, half expecting to see George hovering for a chat, but it's the CEO.

'Can I have a quick word?' he says.

The clicking of Emily's keyboard stops. All my team is staring at us, George's neck being the tallest. The CEO's shoulders are up and slightly back.

His face looks relaxed. My knees are twitching at high speed. We go up the lift in silence. He shuts us in the boardroom annexe office and waves for me to sit down. He waits till I stop shifting.

Then he says, 'Peter has been telling me about your efforts and the pipeline you have created. You will know that, with your dedication, there is considerable opportunity for growth in our business. The numbers show your team's contribution is already 18% of this year's budgeted income. You may have heard on the grapevine that a director position will be vacant later in the year.'

My thumbs are cold, my heart is thudding, and then my nose twitches. It's the familiar smell of cheese.

'The board would like you to take on the role of a shadow director and we will make it permanent, subject to your continued progress.'

The CEO is two inches taller than Peter. He gazes down at me.

'How do you feel about this? There are some duties as director you need to understand.'

I half leap up from my chair but manage to quickly get back down again, hoping he did not notice. I can't get any words out and want a glass of water.

'As you know, this is a big step, and your salary will rise from June, when the role becomes permanent. My assistant will be in touch with the legalities of being a director. Your main role will continue in new product delivery.'

My voice is back, and I find myself doing an involuntary bow: 'I am fully committed to DigiArt. I won't let you or the board down, you have my promise.'

I take the lift straight down. I want to run on the high street. Need to burn energy. It's windy, and I can feel the cool air on my arm. But my chest is warm. My breathing is more normal by the time I reach the coffee shop. The lady beams at me. I want to tell her about my promotion. I order the same cinnamon latte and the last piece of carrot cake in the display. She scans my app and flashes me her best smile. Her eyes are cornflower blue. Her gaze moves to my solid gold bracelet, an heirloom from my grandad, on my right hand. She glanced at my Rolex watch on my left hand the last time I came. I pull both hands down under the counter. When she returns, her cap is wonky, showing more of her blonde hair. I realise she can't be much over twenty. Her head twists towards me.

She says, 'Mr Aman, we are out of cinnamon spice.' Her tone is sweet, like Kaya's. She scans my app again. 'The next coffee or drink is complimentary, Mr Aman. Any size.'

I text my sister first. Then my mum. My mum doesn't understand my career too much. But she will understand my elation. I haven't spoken to her for two weeks. Scrolling on my phone, my hand finds Raff's number. I see my last message to him. It says, *Let's talk more about my promotion next Monday.* Next to it was Raff's reply – a thumbs up.

Raff would have immediately understood this moment. I start typing by instinct. Then I press *delete*. Raff will never read my messages ever. I drop my phone onto the table and gulp the sugar-laced coffee. A few minutes later, my fingers seem to have taken a life of their own and I find myself texting Nabin. I press send and then realise he will be right in the middle of his school lessons.

Back at the office, word is out, no doubt by the CEO's assistant, who tends to leak out gossip in a coordinated way.

Emily wanders across. 'How's your day going, Aman? All well?' she says, her eyes bobbing up and down in anticipation.

I want to savour the moment and wait for the formal communication tomorrow. St Paul's Cathedral looks bigger from the window. The two sparrows that sit on the windowsill chirp as if they are celebrating with me.

At around 4 p.m., I sit inside the bathroom cubicle. I scroll through messages, many of which have thumbs-up emojis. There is a text from Nabin: 😎 *Wow dad. This sounds good* 👍. *Got det. – msg beeped in class … My fault forgot to put on silent* 😔.

***

With the preparation of the director role, my email fills up, and most days, I am lucky if I exit before 7 p.m. That means I skip the late afternoon stroll for a coffee. The clocks moved forward last week, and it's still light when I drive past the coffee shop on my way home. I recognise one of the ladies bringing in the outdoor signage. All their faces look stern and tired.

Raff comes up more and more in my thoughts at night. During the day, I can easily push him out of my thoughts, but he is there in every dream. There is no linearity in my dreams; it's all a jumble, from our time at university to our last conversation or a specific game of squash.

I look up as I pull into the driveway. Nadia and Nabin's room lights are on. Inside, Mona is on the phone talking about scheduling issues at her hospital. A typed letter in an open brown envelope lies on my bed. It is stamped with *Stanmore School* in crimson next to a second-class stamp. It reads: *Dear Mr and Mrs Pradhan, We had arranged a meeting to review the progress of your child Nadia. Both our teachers waited until 7 p.m., as you had requested a late meeting.*

I slap my forehead twice. It was in my diary, and I recall a reminder from my calendar.

Mona sometimes reminds me about school appointments. I have no-one to blame but myself. Nadia had complained of bullying by a girl, and it was something I wanted to bring up with the school. Now, the opportunity is lost.

The rest of the letter continues: *We at Stanmore School take education seriously. Our ethos of Commitment, Kindness and Excellence is enshrined in everything we do. We want to ensure your child has every success in their studies and in their whole personal development. But we need your support.*

I laugh in a splutter. I compare the school's values to those of DigiArt's. I know them by heart, having had to put them in every proposal: *Focus, Attitude and Delivery*. I am glad the CEO doesn't have sight of the teacher's letter.

***

Two weeks later, I bump into the CEO on the lift going down.

'Your hit rate on proposals is well over 70%. It was brought to my attention at a global sales meeting today. What's your magic spell, Aman?' he says with a large smile. 'We are all looking forward to seeing you join the board.'

My neck grows by at least an inch. He steps out of the lift but wedges his foot on the door, causing it to beep rapidly.

He says, 'Not sure how much you come down to the second floor. The supplier's office is a bit dingy, isn't it? But I always like to go and see where the action is.'

With that, he removes his foot and blinks as the door closes.

The next morning, George is more garrulous than normal. He says, pointing to his online *Sun* newspaper, 'Another royal with his pants down. Do they never learn?' He laughs.

'They enjoy the publicity.'

Louis points out that the story has made it to the *Financial Times*, a small section on the bottom left. George continues in full flow with his assumptions about who might have done what. Everyone's feet are pointing at him, apart from mine. His hypotheses are not based on any facts. Worse, everyone on this floor finds him amusing. I stare at the screen, my anger growing towards George. Three days ago, he spent an hour talking about sandwich fillings. Which he then followed by wanting a discussion of the weather in the Mediterranean. He once did a ten-minute monologue on the types of tomatoes he prefers. The thing is, he meets deadlines. I have nothing to pull him up on.

I can't stand the banter anymore. I get the team together earlier than our planned meeting at 11 a.m.

Emily's face has more wrinkles around her mouth than usual. From what I can pick up from George yesterday morning, she had a massive fight with her son on Monday.

I say, 'Even though we know art in general is subjective, my research shows there are genres of art that appeal to different cultures.'

I look at Emily.

'I agree with Aman. My view is that tondos converted to digital can be better suited for the rich in Brazil and Chile. There is something about circular art that works for them.'

The nice thing about Emily is, no matter what her mood, she always has ideas. In fact, she is even more creative when she has a domestic problem. Yet, the dark patches under her eyes are set.

At the end of the meeting, I announce my soon-to-be director role, trying to act as modestly as possible. A couple of the juniors open their eyes wider. George's eyes are squinting. He doesn't even congratulate me and attempts to make a joke about me needing a bigger desk. It's silly – not even original.

Nobody is at home when I get back at 7 p.m. Nabin is at his indoor football training straight from school, and Nadia is at her friend's house. The minute I put on the new LED lights in our kitchen, I see the reflection of a tiny trail of water on the floor. It's right by the cupboard near the sink. Worse still, the inside of the cupboard is damp and starting to crumble. The cheap MDF veneer is something we had not spotted until we moved into the house. A few weeks back, I noticed a bit of dampness in the cupboard when I opened it to grab a kitchen towel but had ignored it in a stupid hope it would go away. I switch off the stopcock and divert the family to have dinner at my mum's house. I order a takeaway, call the plumber and use the nearest hand towel to clear up the mess.

I was intending to spend the evening planning Kaya's wedding. I wanted to fix the order of proceedings and call the manager at the Rayish venue. Plus, there are twenty pages of paperwork to read for my new role.

Within two hours, an emergency plumber has sealed the leaking T-joint and charged a hefty amount. It is all going on my credit card. Five minutes later, after seeing him out, the doorbell rings. The plumber must have left something behind. Instead, I find Kaya at the door. Her car is in the same parking spot that the plumber left. Her unkempt hair worries me.

She steps inside but hovers by the door.

'Uncle, I thought I would come and see you. I have decided to meet you in person. I know you are busy with your promotion and work,' she says, 'but you aren't answering my calls.'

She smiles but I can see the tension around her mouth. Her palms are rolled into half fists. That part of her DNA she must have from my sister. She is rocking her body forward and back.

My sister and I used to get into some huge arguments and neither one of us would give way once we took our stance. I am already deflated with the plumbing leak and have no energy to fight her.

'Uncle, unless we start doing some work on this every week nothing will happen. And you know Remi is no good at these things.'

Remi is Kaya's fiancé.

She continues, 'I don't want to go to a wedding planner, but I am thinking of taking one on.'

Her left eyebrow twitches, like she can sense my guilt.

I want to put my hands in a prayer position and beg her not to do this. A wedding planner, as far as I am concerned, is a waste of time. I can see Grandad shaking his head at me. He is saying, 'Weddings are when family counts.'

The latch clicks and the front door opens. Mona and Nadia come in together. Kaya gives them each a hug, the one to Nadia being the longest. Then, she looks at me.

'Uncle, I'd like you to help me though with the limousine bookings, could you do that?'

She's making a conciliatory offer to dampen my shortcomings.

'Kaya, give me another chance,' I say, my voice stumbling. 'You know how much I want to do this. I promised your mum. It's tradition.'

Her face turns redder. She fist bumps Nadia, bows to Mona and takes out her car keys.

Nadia turns to me the moment the front door closes. Her voice sounds like her tutor.

She says, 'Dad, are you in trouble? Kaya looks very upset. I thought you said everything was on plan. Maybe you should get Uncle Lekh involved.'

I shout, 'Please get off my back, I can manage this, and don't mention Lekh again.'

I head to the kitchen. I start looking for any more leaks inside cupboards. Afterwards, I search for the biggest bar of chocolate in the larder.

My phone pings at 10 p.m. The notification reads: *Based on your recent transaction, your account will be over limit by £350*. A daily charge of £10 will commence tomorrow. Thank God my gold card has a 24-hour service.

The man on the line reminds me of the concierge I met in Dubai. He says, 'Mr Pradhan, with your updated salary, and checking your spending in March, we'd be delighted to increase your borrowing limit to £9,000.'

I work out the sums in my head. The interest payment itself will set me back a few hundred pounds this year. I am spending the family money as quickly as I am contributing to it.

CHAPTER 4

SUPPRESSION

———————————

The next day, my sister Larissa rings. Mona turns off the tap and steps out of the kitchen. The dishwasher door is half open. Mona doesn't like to hear my sister and me bickering. It's midnight in Mauritius, but at only 8 p.m. here, Larissa will still expect my full attention.

My sister doesn't ask how Nadia and Nabin are. 'Kaya is in tears. What did you say to her?' Her voice speeds up. 'You promised me you would take care of the wedding planning.'

She is on speakerphone, making her tone even harsher. 'Kaya wants to get a wedding planner. That's going to cost, but that's not the point.' She comes off the speaker, and I can hear tapping sounds. I imagine her moving up and down her sprawling bungalow.

'Do you remember, Grandad always said a family wedding needs planning by family, not outsiders.' Her voice is more controlled now. 'Last year, you gave me and Mum a fifteen-minute lecture on how weddings should be organised.' Her talking speeds up. 'Do you remember all that? What are you going to do?'

Why does she have to say *remember* twice? I know what's coming next:

'Typical of you. You do this all the time, pretending you know it all with your management fads, but then you let people down. I told Mum that's what would happen.'

I want to tell her that she is the one who uses management fads more than me. I repeat the promises I made yesterday to Kaya. My sister relents but sighs before she says goodbye.

I want to throw my phone into the dishwasher.

***

Today, I attend my first board meeting as Shadow Director. I try to match the serious faces all around; my status on the fourth floor means nothing here. One of the non-executives sits two chairs to my right, and she has my document open on her device.

Hardeep speaks in a soft musical tone like Kaya, yet her eyes are still. 'What will happen if there is a credit crunch in China? Our sales depend on people's sense of wealth, as this allows them to invest in art.'

I don't like my assumptions about growth in the Far East and China being challenged.

All eyes at the oval table are watching me.

I murmur, 'It's something I will look into for risk mitigation and report to the next board meeting.' I want to tell the board about my achievements in the last month.

Next day, I scroll through my unread emails. The one with the subject marked *Cancellation* gets my heart thumping. I roll up my sleeves in reaction. It's the first bad news on the list. One of the contracting parties, in China, has exercised their option to withdraw from the agreement. They have only used the platform for five months. It is a significant loss, as I'd envisaged at least two years of use.

The email says: *We found customer focus is changing to different artwork as they explore more local paintings. The public is becoming nationalistic. As you well know, perceptions are important in our target market. Your platform is great, but needs have changed.*

The following morning, with broken sleep and no breakfast, I get to the office a few minutes after 6:30 a.m. The first light appears from behind the grey clouds, and my car thermometer says 7°C. I fire up my laptop and put the kettle on in the kitchenette. The inside of the fridge has no hint of smell. Everything is arranged in symmetry. I suspect one of the juniors keeps it that way. I call the customer on video. It's after lunch, their time. The man opposite me is friendly but direct. His English grammar is better than mine.

He says, 'I am certain I informed your George about our concerns on sales and the risk of demand drop.'

I can't remember George ever having said this.

After ten minutes, I press the red button and shout out, 'Ugh.' I want to grab George by his collar. I am shaking. The heating is not yet on in the office. My doubts about George were right. I should not have taken his assurance at face value. What else could he be hiding from me?

Waiting two hours for George to arrive is painful. But my anger is not as bad by the time he arrives at 8:49 a.m. I am at his desk as he removes his puffer jacket. We go to the nearest vacant meeting room.

'George, what about the feedback? Why did you not share that they wanted local Chinese paintings as part of their portfolio? This is something we could have done easily, for we have the data sets on this. I am upset about your attitude, George.' I pause for breath. 'We could have saved this account.'

George's face does not flinch by a centimetre. Yet his arms are folded tight. He says, 'I didn't think it was important to mention; it didn't seem like a huge concern to them at the time.' He looks at the ceiling, then says, 'Anyway, these things can happen. There is uncertainty in the Chinese market. And besides, it's a small contract.'

His voice is a lower octave than mine. The heat in my head returns. I want to explode. Suddenly, Raff is in my head. He is warning me that, in my senior role, it would be foolish to attribute blame without following due processes. At the board meeting, we shared a summary of a three-year-old grievance from an old employee … It has cost us a bundle to avoid going to court.

I clench my fist underneath the table as tightly as I can. 'Is there anything else you need to tell me?'

'Nah,' he says.

That is the same word Nadia repeats to me on one of her bad days. I spend the next half hour crafting an email, with the main words being *lessons learnt*, *oversight* and *one-off*, and I send it to Peter.

'Why did I not get a sniff?' echoes in my mind. I find a hiding place in the gents and put my hands on my forehead. I silently say, 'I should have asked more questions and sat in on more meetings.' I want to get hold of Raff for advice, but there is no Raff at the end of a line. His soothing words would have instantly lifted me, and he would have said 'I understand' several times.

Later Emily wanders over to my desk. 'You look troubled,' she whispers. I ask her if she has an ibuprofen. She nods her head to the lift. 'Do you want to have a chat?'

We head out to the coffee place. It's a windy April day, and the sky is near-grey, except for a blob of blue to the east. I wonder if it's near ultramarine, the same colour that is expensive to source in Renaissance paintings. The spots of rain get heavier as we walk along the pavement, which already has water patches. My rain jacket is in the car, and my blazer is gathering darkening blobs, building one at a time. The billboard right next to the coffee shop is the only bright thing around. It has a picture of a man in a suit; he looks like me but with less hair. He has steam coming out of his ears and it says, '*Stress damages you.*' With a subtitle underneath, '*1 in 3 people can develop long-term illnesses.*' It has been there for a while, but this is the first time I gaze at the advert properly. I feel pain in the middle of my chest, and my breathing is heavy.

The lady at the coffee place is ever-present, who, for some reason, I know is from Poland.

She says, 'It's nice to see you again. Would you like an almond latte with cinnamon and an extra shot of espresso?'

I don't like the familiarity. I want to change my mind.

Instead, I say, 'And a double espresso for my colleague.'

As soon as the warmth enters my tummy, my hand stops twitching.

Emily takes out two white pills, passes them over to me, and then takes out her vape. 'Aman, don't be so down. Contracts can get cancelled. It's happened before at DigiArt.' She stretches out her hand and blows on the tip. 'You need to be a bit more, what's the word ... philosophical about these things.'

I say, 'George's reports did not mention even a hint of any problems. We have asked everyone to complete their risk and issue list on your weekly template, but he mentioned nothing. It's a clear risk George should have highlighted.'

'Are you sure the customer is not trying to come up with a lame excuse?'

That makes no sense. George hasn't been forthcoming about what he knows. He has emotional intelligence. That's obvious in the way he socialises, so he should have picked it up. 'I want him out!' My chest hurts a bit more. She puts her hand on my shoulder and taps it.

'Maybe an overnight think will help you make better decisions,' she says.

As we leave the coffee shop, the Polish lady beckons me. She scans my app, doesn't look at me, and is gone by the time I thank her. Even she must have read my mood. The rain outside is pouring harder.

***

Usually, my head is in a good place once I get to the office. Nowadays, it fluctuates. Today, I have an email with a principal *agreement* from our proposal to another company in China. It doesn't lift me, not like winning work did in the past. George remains schtum after I share the news. He usually has a quip every time I make an announcement. But not today. His lips are circled inwards, and his head is closer to his screen. I tap his monitor and say, 'Fancy a brew?' – a term he uses a lot. He looks up, his lips widen, and he pushes back his chair. He lifts both hands in a yawning motion, stretches them further out, then switches off his screen. I go with his choice of Zeno's café. George asks for a pot of tea, and two iced buns. I order a mug of instant coffee. The lady who takes his order has unkempt hair and gives George a flirty grin as she clicks the till buttons. The place looks exactly the same as it did on my last visit two years ago. The tatty menu has stuck-on labels with adjusted prices. It's packed with a humming, noisy atmosphere, a different aura to my coffee shop. This place has music piped from a radio station and just two coffee options. The staff are all my age or older. Plus, the walls are plain vanilla, with a misaligned picture of a fruit basket. It looks like it's been bought from a car boot sale.

George sips his tea and plays with the bowl of sugar. My mix, in a large unbranded white mug, tastes surprisingly nice with the thick iced bun. The iced buns sit on plates made of stiff recyclable paper, resting on a table with unsteady legs.

'I am sorry for my outburst the other day. I was just disappointed about the contract loss.'

He waves his hand like it's nothing. We both look down for a few seconds.

I continue, 'But I do find you take things too casually. We have customers to serve, and we need discipline in our work. It winds me up a lot when you think everything should be fun.'

He looks into my eyes, examining my honesty. His chest fills with air. He says, 'You think I don't care, but I do. I won't let work take over my life, Aman. My dad died in an industrial accident. He was working a second shift, real tired, and didn't follow the safety stuff. It was entirely his fault, but was it because he was overworked? Who knows?'

I open my mouth, yet he continues.

'You take everything so seriously and want to blame someone. You keep saying that there is a root cause, but sometimes there is no root cause to things going wrong. Shit happens. Let's take the contract loss with that customer. I had no idea it was coming. They were all fine with it. I even asked them about their worries. But sometimes, things hit us out of nowhere, and none of your risk-planning methods can avoid it. Remember the bloke in the US – Rumsfeld – he talked about *unknown unknowns*. That's why I take bad news in a more relaxed way than you.'

I take a spoonful of sugar from the bowl and pour it back in. Its colour is pure white.

I say, 'You know, my grandad once said the true reasons for some events may be completely hidden from us and remain a mystery. But my telecoms degree told me there was always a root cause. We just have to dig deeply to find it.'

He looks down into his half-empty mug and pushes it away. The table creaks. Then he says, 'My dad died when I was fifteen and I didn't get a chance to go to a posh uni like you, having to slave away after GCSEs. But I do know my stuff, mate. In fact, Peter told me joining your team would help smooth out your rough edges.'

My right foot has a tremor. I want to get up and run; I don't like personal chats with office staff. The piped song finishes, and an advert comes on. It's about some natural sleeping pills, apparently with no side effects.

I say without any thought, 'Thanks for clearing the contract issue ... let's continue this discussion later.'

The table makes a grating noise as we both get up. I make an excuse about going to the gents. As I wash my hands, I realise I didn't even acknowledge the loss of his dad. I can't go back to the office. In seven minutes, I find myself at the entrance to the park.

The grass is full of rain from the day before, but patches are beginning to dry. I walk on the circular path avoiding two worms. The lady I met two months ago is on the same bench reading a leaflet. I sit down but look in the opposite direction. Yet, within a minute, my gaze wanders towards her. Her right pupil shifts like she's expecting me.

'Isn't it amazing the number of oak trees preserved in the park? That's why the magpies like coming here.'

I never knew the black-and-white birds were called magpies. Pigeons were the only birds I recognised. I wonder why I am so ignorant about nature.

She puts the leaflet in her tiny brown satchel and continues, 'It's a little dance isn't it, between birds and trees.' She looks at me. 'Things carry on, don't they, even whether we are there or not?'

'I suppose they do,' I respond. I want to say, *I was out for a week from the office when I was in Dubai and my team struggled to make decisions.*

'I sometimes feed the birds,' she continues. 'Only seeds not bread, but if I didn't someone else would.'

'There are some jobs few can do,' I retort, somehow glad of this conversation.

'Yes, I suppose you are right. But, if the experts aren't there, perhaps the need goes away? I mean, pigeons for example, on that birch tree.'

She points to a tree, tall and thin without many leaves. It's ten metres to the left of us and has four pigeons on it.

She continues, 'If no-one fed them here, they'd fly off elsewhere and find more natural sources of food, don't you agree?'

I am enjoying this tussle. I say, 'You make a good point, but it's different in my case.' I explain what I do, like I am reading my LinkedIn profile.

The old lady's ears raise up.

'If I didn't run these projects, then who would? It's taken me years to build the expertise. It's a bit of a craft, to be honest. Like tying up our IT infrastructure, the market of digitised paintings and dealing with ambiguous customer needs.'

'Yes, of course you are valuable,' she says and then, with a pause, continues, 'but is the work of utmost value to you?'

I nod but want to laugh.

An old man opens the gate on the other side of the park. He has the same build as my grandad, short and compact. When I was twelve, my grandad and I went to the market every week and sometimes to the library. Every so often, he would say something cryptic. Sometimes it made sense, but sometimes it was nonsense. I used to nod like I understood. The magpies move closer to us, pecking in the grass.

She removes the leaflet from her purse. She says, 'Since you know so much about technology, do you think it's worth getting nano broadband?'

I scan the document and give her my advice and some possible options.

'Bless you,' she says with wonky lips. She stands up, picks up her stick, and turns around to say, 'Hope I see you again.'

She waves her stick twice and walks at an even pace. I watch her reach the opposite entrance to the park, which comes out onto a suburban street. She turns back and waves her stick towards me one last time. My tummy is stirring, and I shake my head. I hope I see the old lady again.

The Tuesday after, I find myself wide awake, my neck covered in sweat, and see the clock says 2:42 a.m. in bright green. Tonight, my dream is more vivid. I see my grandad reading my eulogy at my funeral, saying, 'Aman will be most remembered for his hard work delivering Cloud projects.' Everyone's gaze is downwards, but no-one is crying. Nabin is on his Xbox and Nadia is chatting with her friend. Kaya is in her wedding *sārī,* and my sister is in her work suit. My wife is nowhere to be seen. Raff is there at the front, but his eyes are on a painting at the back of the crematorium.

It has been five months since Raff's death. I have lost count how many times I jolt up between 2 and 3 a.m. Raff appears like he is alive in every dream. We are usually walking together, but I can't remember the words he uses. And once I wake up, I can't sleep again, with Raff, my childhood, my work and my future all jumbled up.

Mona lifts her head an inch from the pillow and mumbles, 'Stop moving around.' She presses the small button on top of the clock. 'It's 3 a.m. Try and get some sleep.' She puts her hand on my back.

A minute later, I can hear the whistle of air leaving her mouth. I want to adjust my pillow again, but it will disturb Mona. That joy of my promotion, our 5-star holiday in Dubai and a gold credit card now mean nothing. Even the respect of colleagues is meaningless. I despise all the flies in my head.

At 7 a.m., the alarm goes off. I don't put it on snooze anymore. The act of sitting up lessens the buzz of flies in my head. I have a new routine. A double espresso within ten minutes of getting up becomes my habit. My breakfast is one piece of toast and sugary marmalade. That combination keeps my mind concentrated, at least for the morning.

At 7.45 a.m. by the door, I find an A4 brown envelope without a stamp. The letterbox clink from last night now holds meaning. The envelope is marked *URGENT – Hand Deliver*. On the left-hand side is the school emblem, a new updated design with more rounded edges. I jump into my car and throw the letter on the passenger seat and prepare myself for any possible bad news. At the last traffic light, I can bear it no longer. I rip the envelope open in the middle, force the paper out and give the first page a scan.

Dear Mr and Mrs Pradhan, we would like you to meet Ms Parker, our Head of Student Welfare, on Friday 03 May at 10:30 a.m. Your daughter, Nadia, has been on our behaviour code E four times. This has been due to bullying. It is important that you …

A car hoots from behind. I throw the pieces of paper on the passenger seat. The press of the accelerator makes all the paper disperse across the seat, and some on the floor. I press my thumb hard against the volume button on the wheel. When I arrive, all the paper has found its way to the passenger floor. I ignore it; all my remaining energy is to get me through the workday.

Nowadays, my concentration levels are fine till about midday; after that, I can't read more than two paragraphs at a time on contracts and proposals. I can't seem to absorb all the words; the jargon blurs in my head. It means I skip details and go with my intuition. But I can understand the numbers that show the sales figures and the margin on each project. Every time we achieve something at work, my depression lifts for an hour, sometimes two. It's been like this for weeks, but worse than that, I am expecting it tomorrow and the week after.

But today after the letter from the school, there are more flies inside.

In the evening, I sit in the kitchen, spreading all the paper on the table, and read everything in the letter twice. Nadia is in her room. Mona arrives fifteen minutes after me. My wife arranges the bits of paper back in order and then shakes her head as her finger traces each line. Her eyes are furrowed. She says, 'Surprising to me. Nadia's never mentioned anything.'

Nadia opens her door after two knocks. She is sitting up and texting someone on her phone. I point to the opening paragraph. The paper is already looking dog-eared. She turns pale red. Her eyes dart top to bottom across the first page, and her mouth is open.

'Is this true, Nadia? Have you been bullying someone?' asks Mona.

Nadia shakes her head a full 180 degrees like she did when she was a child. Her throat is moving, and her eyes are blinking. She reads the last page with the word *bullying* in bold.

Half a minute later, she responds, 'Of course not! This is crazy. Ishita is bullying meeee ... And she stole my Montblanc pen. I saw her put it into her bag.'

Mona's face looks horrified. It must be a mirror of my face.

'Dad, I told you about a girl who was a bully, now she has turned all her attention to me. She told me the other day that I was like an odd-shaped tree. I can't help it if I am tall.'

Nadia had mentioned some teasing a few weeks back. I had put it down to school banter.

Nadia spends another fifteen minutes discussing all the petty incidents with this girl, Ishita. But it doesn't shed more light on the situation. Maybe the school has got it all wrong, but we won't be able to avoid the meeting.

Back in the kitchen, I say, 'The last incident I remember was a boy at the nursery who had pulled her hair, and in retaliation, she kicked him.'

Mona's eyes open wider. 'And don't you remember, in primary school, she was warned about her aggressiveness with one teacher? But we put it down to the poor social skills of the teacher.'

'Nadia does have a feisty nature when confronted. Maybe we have ignored this part of her too much. I mean, I hardly ever see it.'

Mona's shoulders drop back. 'Don't feel so guilty. It could be a one-off incident. Look at you with your head in your hands, you are taking this all too seriously.' She strokes my back. 'I will take time off, so we can both go. My boss owes me some favours.'

I remove the picture of a three-year-old Nadia stuck with a magnet on the fridge door. 'She has been rather quiet in the last few months, but with my duties at work, I have not given any attention to this.'

I turn towards Mona and let out a short laugh.

'I remember walking her to the library every Saturday from when she was three. We would talk about lamp-posts, the colour of people's doors and the wonky pavement. And we always chatted to the grey-haired stocky man who always walked his dog around 3 p.m. Even then, she would tell me her likes and dislikes and what upset her. And one day, she must have been seven, she had taken a lollipop from the shop and put it in her pocket.'

Mona laughs. 'She was quiet for three days and then told me about the incident while we were removing some weeds from the garden.' She looks up.

I say, 'Oh yeah, and then we had our first chat about the difference between stealing and sharing. It's the first time I got upset with her.'

I had taken Nadia back to the shop the next weekend to fess up. We had bought two more lollipops from the shopkeeper, and I had narrated the parable about stealing that I learnt from Grandad to Nadia. I remember my words: 'Better to share things than to take what belongs to others.'

Not that I agreed with Grandad. I am not sure I would share my expertise in art tech with anyone, and nobody in the world could drive my car.

Mona taps my hand and pushes her chair back. 'You never show too much anger, do you? You hide it and when it comes out, you erupt. Just like Nadia.'

Friday comes around in a blink, and we find ourselves in a classroom with the teacher, Ms Parker. She is sitting on one of the children's desks, with Nadia opposite her. She is petite and slim and looks twenty-five but with the way her chin juts she must be older. There are two vacant chairs next to Nadia's. I haven't been inside a classroom in twenty-two years. The walls are full of colourful charts, acronyms and phrases. One wall is about geography, showing a map of Asia. I can see the Himalayan range and Nepal underneath. The other is about physics and has a statement attributed to Newton written inside a thought cloud, *What goes up must come down*. I hope that is not always true in all contexts. The last wall says, *Studying technique*. Underneath it says, *Examine, Evaluate and Engage*. That sounds clever. I want to use that phrase at work.

The room seems bigger than when I went to school, and nothing appears broken. At work, we have a desk with its footrest missing, which makes it wobbly. Ms Parker goes out of the room to answer an urgent call. Nadia excuses herself to go to the bathroom. Her face is turning red.

When Nabin and I came to visit the school two years ago, he said, 'I like this school, Dad. I couldn't see chewing gum under any desks when I went round three classrooms.' I run my hands under my table and then look underneath the desk next to us. There is nothing there but bare wood.

Ms Parker moves slowly, but in one motion, like a swan, she returns to her seat. Nadia's senior teacher can't be taller than five feet. Yet, her upright posture gives her a confident presence that makes her look like a compact tower. She looks at me and I look at the wall on her left.

Nadia returns and her face still has a glint of water, but her eyes are less red.

Ms Parker starts. 'As I stated in my letter, Nadia has been bullying a girl. We have warned her a few times. The incidents are numerous and have gotten worse in the last month.'

I can't believe the teacher used the word *gotten*; must be a generational thing.

She reads through the evidence, 'This included swearing at her, calling her "fat" and "idiot", which have been so numerous we have lost count in our records. On one occasion, she called Ishita a "stupid tart" and showed her fist in the playground.'

Ms Parker is completely still as she repeats the foul language. My hands are in two fists under the table, and I want to chew some gum. Nadia is rocking her chair. Her eyes are hard. I didn't know she had been in detention after school six times this term. Mona's gaze is darting back and forth from the teacher to Nadia. My daughter has the occasional tantrums. Yet, at her karate classes, the sensei mentioned how kind she is and how she is willing to help others with some of their kata moves.

I lean forward to make a statement. Before I can say anything, Ms Parker looks at Nadia and nods.

Nadia fires with, 'She is the one who is b ... b ... bullying me. She gets her friends to pick on me, so she looks like a goodie. Worse than that, she says nasty things to me when nobody is there. On Monday, she told me she would get me expelled.'

Nadia starts crying and we have a minute's pause. Ms Parker's body moves a few millimetres. Her grey eyes are soft. Nadia stems her tears and trots out more ugly language and threats she has experienced. Once Nadia becomes repetitive, Ms Parker comes back in.

She says, 'We have talked to Ishita as well, about her behaviour, but that doesn't excuse your own, Nadia.' She scans all three of us. 'What do you think we can do to help Nadia make better choices for her future?'

On the table, I can see she has a list of her own, but I can't read it upside down. I wonder if my retaliation to George in the office would be construed as bullying.

There is a reconciliation meeting arranged between Nadia and Ishita and two commitments on behaviour.

Ms Parker spent most of her time laying out facts and getting acceptance, not forcing action. I look around the classroom walls again. In my corporate world, most time is spent on actions rather than awareness. Facts are used only to support decisions.

Ms Parker finishes with, 'I wanted to remind you of our school values – commitment, kindness, and excellence. With this in the mind of students and parents, things can be better for all.'

I want to shake Ms Parker's hand, but her right hand is glued to the door handle. She does give Nadia two taps on her shoulder. I expected her to have a private word with us. In the office, I am used to being pulled aside by a peer to talk about 'people problems' or get to grips with internal politics.

On our journey back home, Nadia's head is sticking out between the two front seats. 'I want to restart my karate class. Can you take me please, Dad, on Thursdays, now your squash has stopped with Uncle Raff? My friend is going so we could share pickups with her dad.'

I have not seen her this enthusiastic for a while. I agree on the spot.

When we get home, Mona asks for a mini conference in the kitchen. She says, 'We are not spending enough time with Nadia or Nabin for that matter.' She scrolls through her calendar. 'I am going to talk to my boss and take some time off. It would be nice if you can take some time off at half-term.'

I look at my calendar and wave my phone. 'Look, my work diary is full with back-to-back meetings. Plus, I need lots of time for the preparation of the three Chinese proposals. There is also a chance I may have to fly out to China at half-term. Our new agent wants to organise a conference in Shanghai.'

Mona's eyes have narrowed into a thin oval shape. Her corneas and pupils are dark. I have seen this look twice in our seventeen years of marriage. One of those was when I had not called her mum when she was unwell and in hospital. She closes her eyes and waves her head.

'I think our daughter's happiness matters more than your career.'

Her eyes are piercing my chest, focusing on the wall behind me. 'You told me your father spent too much time at work, which hurt your relationship. Didn't you say that you felt a gap in your life because of this?'

I fire back, 'I can't remember saying that. Anyway, this has nothing to do with my dad. I want the next promotion. Look what it gave us – the Dubai trip. And the Turkey 5-star experience before that. Was that not all wonderful?'

'Yes, it was, but something cheaper would have given us the same pleasure. I found some of the opulence in Dubai too much. 22k is the pay for one of my administrative assistants.'

My forehead is thumping. 'But I thought you said you loved it.'

She sighs, her eyes still narrow. 'I love our daughter's happiness more. And since we are at it, you never listen to a word I say. As soon as I talk about my problems, you look away. You know I love your ambition, but this is crazy. Has Raff's death not shown you how short life is? You haven't even paused to reflect and have just suppressed everything.'

I hear myself saying, 'I am sorry.'

Her eyes are normal now, but her voice is breaking up. 'I am going to go and spend a few days with my mum this half-term. You don't listen to me; you are not interested in anything I say. I am fed up.'

Mona is crying now. She stands up, wanting a hug. I want to run away but I hold her briefly before she pulls away.

I sit down and put my face in my hands. She pushes her chair in place. I hear the latch click behind me.

My calendar has red, blue and orange marks for the next three weeks. I had forgotten half-term was coming up. Any big changes to my diary now will alert Peter for sure. I massage the top of my forehead and grab a bar of chocolate. I open social media and search for the juiciest comments. A politician is caught on a tax evasion charge. That distracts me for the next hour.

During dinner, Mona ignores me and talks only to the kids about a mystery series that they are watching on Netflix. At about 8:30 p.m. I sweep the high-density wooden floor of our kitchen. The kids are in the living room and Mona is chatting to someone on the phone at the top of the staircase.

The doorbell rings followed by a loud knock, like all couriers do. I don't like their impatience. A uniformed courier is outside. She has a package in her hands with the words in gilded letters *Gold Card Holder* on top. The rectangular package can mean many possibilities. I open it straight away and get rid of the filling material as fast as possible.

Inside is a small bottle of whisky, with a handwritten card with the words: *Your reward for 7,000 points*. I move the bottle to the small larder inbuilt into our kitchen and step back. I want to drink the bottle right now.

It's Saturday morning. I sit in the warm kitchen. My body is soothed by my giant mug of tea, but my mind is like a sinusoidal wave. Mona has had to go to the dentist and Nadia is out with her friends. Nabin's football game is cancelled today. I have made a promise to myself not to scroll through social media or check emails today. Instead, I am reading the menu on the takeaway pizza pamphlets and comparing the two brands.

Nabin walks in, and I mumble a hello, my eyes remaining on the pizza pamphlet. Both have options for different family sizes and budgets, and they all have money-off offers. I turn the leaflet around. One's call for action is it's *guaranteed delivery in 20 minutes*, and the other's is a *free bottle of Coke* for any family-size order.

'Dad, the fluorescent light underneath the cupboard is forever flickering. I wonder what it could be?'

He comes up close to me.

I put down the leaflet. I reply, 'Nabin, fluorescent lights don't last due to the gas in them.'

Nabin stays close. I get up to have a look and both ends are a patchy black, a sign of a defect.

'Dad, shall we go to the shop on Morpeth Road? The model says it is an R70. It's a large shop; they will have it.'

My body doesn't want to move beyond the kitchen. Yet within a few minutes, we are in the car as we head out to the shop which is a seven-minute drive away. Nabin wants to place the order and chats with the lady at the counter. She returns with a tube lamp. Nabin wiggles his body in excitement.

Back home, Nabin uses his phone flashlight, while I fit the lamp. It's a difficult squeeze, and with my heavy hands, one of the pins on the right side of the lamp breaks.

'Damn!' I yell out in frustration.

Nabin looks at the broken pin and then at me. His face turns into a frown. For a second, I want to call our builder, but that would hurt. Instead, I head back to the shop on my own, my pulse racing as I open the large shop door. The same lady is at the counter and has a wry smile as I show her the broken lamp.

'It's a common problem,' she says. 'Did your son break it? Tell him he needs to be gentler.'

I take responsibility and the lady shrugs. Good thing there is no-one else in the shop.

As soon as I get back in the car, I have a surge of energy. I am going to fix this lamp, no matter what. Nabin doesn't wait for the front door to close.

'Dad, I looked on YouTube. RepairJo says that there's not enough space in the lug gap for the pins to go in.' He has a pointed screwdriver from the toolbox. 'I notice the spring-loaded end on the left of the fitting is not as flexible as the other side.'

I carefully open the fitting to give enough space to the tube light. Under the watchful eye of Nabin, I manage to snap the tube light in. I pray for no damage. Is this how surgeons operate? Nabin turns on the main switch, but there is no fluorescence. I thump my palm on the kitchen top. Nabin gazes directly at me, his dark eyes even more black.

'Dad, you have said that sometimes solving one problem causes another. Do you think we have blown a fuse?'

'It's not possible, Nabin,' I say, finding my calm voice. 'There is a single fuse for all the lights in the kitchen, and the other lights work fine.'

We both look again at the fitting. Nabin says, 'Look, Dad you have jolted the power cable next to the light, and the connection has come away.'

I press the connector in, and the light comes on with the toggle switch. It makes me blink. I shout, 'Yeah!' and then high-five Nabin.

His eyes are narrow. 'Well done Dad.'

Nabin helps me gather the tools and is out of the kitchen before I close the toolkit. I picture him giving me a score of six out of ten for my shoddy work. My shoulder flinches. At the moment, getting my son's appreciation beats getting Peter's nod on winning work.

I close the waste bin and notice the small, thin wooden plinth covering the bottom of the washing machine is wonky by about 30 degrees. How long has it been like this, and why has no-one noticed? It's not on the repair list. When I remove the panel, I see a small bracket has slipped off from its holding. With a tiny adjustment to the bracket with my narrow screwdriver, it fits back on perfectly. I step back. The panel looks perfectly horizontal. I want to show it to Nabin but asking him to come out of his bedroom will annoy him. In celebration, I promise myself a syrup-laden coffee this afternoon.

***

I dread the car journey home from work. It is when any positive feelings from work disappear. Nowadays, memories of Raff are even stronger than the days when he died. Even the Lab4+ audio system in my Mercedes can't distract my thoughts. Raff and I often chatted on our separate ways home when our drive times coincided. Each time we spoke, it was like a clearing of thoughts, to make sense of each other's state. At the zebra crossing, a man is dressed in a football shirt, which is also black and white. On the back it says Chiswick Football Club. After we moved to London, Chiswick is where my sister and I would go to the *Bāhā*. The last time would have been around twenty years ago. I never enjoyed the sermon part, I just found it boring. But I did find myself feeling happier every time I left the *Bāhā* ...

Apart from Mona, I have no-one to share my troubles with. I look down. My stomach is poking out in front of me. My belt is now on its last hole, up two notches from the most worn one. I have not done any exercise for the last five months.

As I switch off the ignition, I see our neighbour, John, opening his front door. I try and remove the crumple on my jacket, as I retrieve it from the back seat.

'Alright?' he asks from a few metres away.

I step away from the car and open the car boot. I try to look busy. John has a drill in his hand and the same soiled blue he wears when doing DIY work. I can hear the hum of his machines at least once a week more in the summer. John gave me some great DIY tips when we moved to this house five years ago and helped me put up a shelf in the garage. I don't want to talk to him. I wave my hand and keep moving towards my front door.

His boy, two years younger than Nabin, had thrown rubbish into our garden four years ago. I banged on his door, and we exchanged words. Since then, all we ever exchanged were a few mumbles. Worse than that, it hurt Nabin. I had forbidden him to play with the boy.

Mona and the kids are out shopping for clothes and the house is quiet, bar the hum of the fridge. I change into my most comfortable T-shirt. My mind flits like a see-saw. I imagine myself opening the bottle of whisky, drinking it and then using mouthwash to hide any smell. Suddenly, from the east, I hear the growing sound of an ambulance siren as it passes to the next street. It fades as it goes down the main A road. The last time I rang 999 was for an ambulance for my dad when he had his final relapse. The image of the hospital scan printed on light pink paper, showing his dilapidated liver with dark marks, is so clear. I open the larder door and don't look on the top shelf. That's where the bottle is. I unwrap the dark luxury chocolate, branded Hotel Chocolat and shaped like an Easter egg. A gift Nadia got from her friend a few weeks back. My daughter will not take long to notice it's all gone. I will think of an excuse later.

The loss of Raff has made my mind permanently ill. It always gets worse as the day goes on.

That evening, I look through the glass-panelled kitchen door. Mona is painting a mandala on an empty jar. Her hands are flowing in a perfect circle. I open the door and close it, trying to make no noise. She doesn't look up. Mona's cheeks are shiny and raised in a manner that tells me she is absorbed in her work. She has overcome Raff's passing quicker than me.

I pull the chair out like I am in an interview. 'I can't seem to shake this feeling of loss and emptiness. Every day is the same. I am not getting better.'

She puts down her paintbrush that is covered in deep blue and dips a fresh one into the light green pot. She glances at me and then starts drawing an inner circle.

'Aman, I understand how you feel. It will take time. But you seem to be going into a shell. You have lost interest in everything, including the kids. We need you as well. Why don't we go to crazy golf this weekend? It's getting warmer and we will all get some fresh air.'

She puts down her paintbrush and holds her gaze at me.

I get up from my chair and check the charge on my phone.

'I am not in the mood for golf,' I say. I picture myself coming last, being beaten by the family. Brooding, Instagram, art photos, Raff's memories and now chocolate, have become my solace.

She shrugs her shoulders. 'Whenever you want me, I am here.'

The next day on my drive, the radio buzzes with news of a credit crunch in China. In the office, Louis has the *Financial Times* front page open on his laptop. He points and reads out the headline: *Shortage of Credit Rocks China*. I love the way he says shortage in his American accent.

I say, 'It's unlikely to be anything that will affect us. Rich people consume no matter what.'

George's giant frame comes towards us. 'I think this thing in China could affect us badly. I mean, I read in *The Sun* that when the

US sneezes we get a cold, but when China sneezes the whole world gets the flu,' he says, laughing at his own joke.

Louis flicks the screen to page three. 'He has a point. We have so many requests from the Far East. According to the FT, there is some risk, but it looks like the authorities are dealing with it by printing money.'

That afternoon, I am at the risk review meeting with other managers. The East comes up as the third point. My shoulders sink. I can feel my breath getting heavier.

I say, 'The risk dimension of impact looks low and there is no reason for any big mitigation. The authorities will control this for sure. We must plough full steam ahead in the Far East. Our bigger risks are the downtime of platforms and competitors. We should worry whether our suppliers can digitise fast enough.'

About half of the managers nod in agreement, and no-one objects.

That evening, after everyone is in bed, my feet are up on our longest sofa. On the mantelpiece opposite is the award *Tech. Visionary – runner-up* from the International Cloud Awards. It took place three years ago on the forty-seventh floor of a Canary Wharf tower. I want to throw the plaque in my grey Ikea bin. Instead, I get up and turn the carved piece of wood around and slouch back into the sofa, staring at its bare back.

CHAPTER 5

THE DOWNFALL

———

About a week later, I wake up to the sound of wardrobe doors opening and closing. From my bed, I see Mona putting a pair of jeans into a large suitcase ... I sit up and remember it's Friday.

I say, 'What are you doing?'

She goes to the wardrobe and pulls out a dress. Her back is all that's visible.

She says, 'I am going to my mum's. Nadia and Nabin are joining me.'

She zips the bag to close it and then opens it again. 'I am sure you can cope fine. And anyway, you don't have much time for us.'

She turns her face to me briefly and then back to her bag. 'You won't miss us.'

I get to the edge of the bed. It feels like I am in a large pit that is swallowing me up. I lost Raff, and now my wife is going too. I move three steps towards her.

I say, 'You can't leave me. We can sort things out.'

My throat is near-dry. 'You can't take my kids away.'

She puts the folded skirt down, puts her finger to her mouth and then starts laughing. Her feet come nearer.

'It's half-term from today, you fool. I told you I'd go and see my mum.' She clenches my hand and kisses me on the cheek. 'You look petrified, Aman.'

She stops laughing. 'I think it will be good for you to have a break from us for a while. You can mull things over without any distraction.' She holds up her summer skirt, the one she looks good in.

I let out a short laugh but want to cry. One part of me wants to be alone. Anyway, Mona's not going to change her mind.

That day, the front desk is adorned by a big, animated graphic. It says *Good luck for the wedding* on the 50-inch digital screen on the wall behind. So, the receptionist is getting married next week. It triggers me on Kaya's impending wedding. There is not a single card on her desk. Those days stopped a few years ago. No doubt she has a digital wedding site on the Cloud, full of personalised and creative messages. All our wedding cards are somewhere in the loft. Messages from aunts, uncles and handwritten letters from three cousins in Nepal.

No-one is on the fourth floor yet. When I get to my desk, I don't bother to pull out my laptop. Instead, I type a WhatsApp message: *Kaya, I wanted to give you an update. From now on, I am going to spend an hour a day on the wedding. I am already looking to check out the venues this weekend.*

That evening, I arrive home just after 7 p.m. Mona's car is not there. None of the house lights are on. There is a message on the kitchen table on the back of the pizza pamphlet:

I waited till 6 p.m., but didn't want to drive too much in the dark. There is curry in the fridge. And a mushroom pie in the freezer. Don't forget to empty the washing machine. The kitchen tap is dripping. Think it needs a washer. Hope you get a chance to reflect without having us around. L U. ♡

On Saturday morning, the sun is hard at work, trying to get light into my house. I stare at the Botticelli painting *Mars and Venus* on my landing. It is the first time I spot the wasps in the picture. They must be buzzing to awaken Mars from his slumber. Venus' eyes are glancing, giving me an order. It forces me to open the curtains.

I came across Botticelli's work during a special exhibition. I was twenty-seven. I had arrived early at our meeting place in Trafalgar Square for a boys' night out and drifted into the National Gallery. I remember his painting; it was not too far from the entrance. It showed a street scene from Florence. It captivated me – the perfect symmetry, the idealistic layout of buildings and the mesmerising colours. Ten years ago, I had bought on impulse a replica of *Mars and Venus*. It's only when I joined my current company that I realised it was by the same Botticelli.

As I step outside the front door, the postman appears in his khaki shorts and red top. He has a letter in his hand. He thrusts it into mine. The signage on the back tells me it's from Nadia's school. I wait till the postman is out of sight. I want to throw it in the blue bin by my back door. Instead, I post it into my letterbox.

An hour and a half later, I find myself outside the National Gallery. A slightly warm feeling comes to my heart. The weight on my mind is lifted but I know it will return. I am glad I am here now. Botticelli's *Mars and Venus* is out on loan to the Uffizi. I couldn't care less. I have the replica at home. Nearby is the Titian section. The *Bacchus and Ariadne* painting confronts me as soon as I enter the room. The painting has about a dozen people standing closely around it. All are with notebooks or smart devices. Every person is older than me and almost all are women. One of them sits down on the floor. Her open page has a scribbled title – *Titian Interest Group*.

I can just about read the plaque: *Bacchus, God of Wine, is returning from a triumphal visit to India, accompanied by his rowdy throng of followers. Here, he sees Ariadne and there is love at first sight.* I check on my AI – the Greeks had conquered parts of India but never made it to Nepal. I stare at the ultramarine blue as the background sky. That colour was expensive at the time and that is why it was so valued. I have seen a Buddha bust with its hair painted in this exact colour at Mum's house. She told me that this blue signified healing and strength. My grandad asked me to pray in front of it before my first A-Level exams. I have never seen the bust again.

I move my body around almost full circle to see where I can go next. As I enter the room to my far right, I see the outline of a painting by Holbein. No-one is in front of it. It shows two men, well groomed and in regal wear. Without reading the plaque I know it's called *The Ambassadors*. In between them are two tiers of objects. At the top is a celestial globe and other objects of astronomy. The meaning is obvious. It shows ambition by reaching up. The shelf below has a stringed instrument with a broken string and a book showing the opening of some hymn. Is this saying life is not that straightforward – does the song signify some joining of threads of life? That's what it is saying to me. At the bottom is an elongated skull, not obvious. The couple of times I have seen the painting before, I always ignored the skull. As far as I was concerned, it was just a joke from Holbein. But now it's saying that failure is always close and maybe even death is near.

I remember the sermon I went to when I was twelve. The monk said that all souls are reborn to another life and our next life will be dependent on our deeds. My grandad told me that some souls get nirvana – an escape from this cycle. But I always hoped I would be reborn.

The skull is more noticeable as I stand at the edge of the painting. I look at the picture of the well-robed men. The picture at first glance is of self-satisfaction; now I see sadness inside their exquisite embellishments.

My visits to any art galleries are few and far between and are normally quick rushes to the Renaissance section. Today, I have an empty home to return to. I take two lefts and a right. The first picture that holds my attention is the one called *Anguish* by Schenck. I have never seen this painting before. Underneath it is a plaque: *On loan until February from the National Gallery of Australia*. It shows a healthy mother sheep full of wool, mourning the loss of its young one, who she is standing over.

My mum always says I look well, even on days when I feel terrible. The background is a harsh winter landscape and there is snow everywhere. There are crows, black and tinged with grey, hovering on the ground, waiting to feast. More crows seem to be arriving in the distance. Both my eyes are moist. I ask the security guard for the nearest exit. He gestures left. A trickle escapes from my left eye. He looks at my cheek for a second and wanders away, his face unmoved.

All the way on the tube, I keep thinking about the picture of the sheep and what it means. Is the young sheep meant to be Raff or is it Nadia? But as soon as I get home, I remember the letter. I leave my shoes on and tear open the letter. My heart is beating rapidly, and my cheeks are full of air. The letter reads: *'Mr and Mrs Pradhan, we wanted to let you know that there has been a significant improvement in your daughter's behaviour. Here at Stanmore School, our values are important. I am sure that, with your support, we can put this episode behind Nadia.* I haven't been home alone for a long time. I shout 'Yaa' and do a mock shiver.

That night, I can't sleep at all. The burst of light from visiting the gallery has disappeared. My grandad, dad, Raff, Kaya and Peter all appear in my dream. We are watching some sheep in the fields. Then, they all look at me and point in the distance. But I can't remember a single word. The *Anguish* painting keeps flashing up. The healthy sheep from that picture is losing all its wool. Its face morphs into one that looks like mine. My head feels crushed and locked in a way that I can't move no matter how hard I try.

On Tuesday after lunch, I receive a message. It says, *I think Kaya is struggling with wedding preparations. She has asked me for help. Shall we have a meet-up to discuss everything? It may be better than trying to do things piecemeal?* My collar is getting warm. I stare at the screen in front of me. What does Lekh know about planning anything? He works at the council pushing paper. And who contacted him – was it Kaya or my sister? I unwrap the sandwich on my desk. I can't taste what's inside and afterwards, put the empty wrapper under my screen. My mind is racing. Part of me wants to text Lekh and say, 'It would be great to help Kaya together, brother.' The other part wants to delete his message, like he didn't exist.

That afternoon, I find an empty meeting room on the third floor. I make an excuse to cancel my meeting with Emily. At 5 p.m. I send Kaya a message: *Here is the shortlist of venues. I have rated them based on all the criteria we agreed on. Once you take a look at these we can go and see the shortlisted three. PS. Your uncle Lekh been in touch. Are you sure you want him involved?*

***

Yesterday, on the top floor, I witnessed a heated discussion between Peter and the CEO. I have never seen Peter look so animated. I would have shared my observations with Raff, and he would have given his analysis of what might be happening.

Later that week, at my catch-up with Peter, his brow has deeper furrows. He is spinning his pen between his thumb and second finger. The hair around his ears has new grey tints. He puts his pen down. It's pointing at me. He leans forward.

'Our top two legacy clients are not going to renew their contracts. You remember they don't have exclusive contracts with us? They are getting their own platforms for digital art. And then selling directly to the public.' He looks at the ceiling. There is a small bead of sweat on his brow.

He says, 'Despite our great relationship with clients, the art galleries started to go direct.'

He shakes his head. 'You need to relook at your portfolio for threats. Your service is for new markets and algorithms for digital slicing. I am worried about risks and less about revenue.'

My mind is in a whizz. A board meeting is coming up. Some difficult questions will be asked. I write the word *Threats* on my device and draw a rectangle around it.

I remember one sermon at the *Bāhā*. I was a teenager, and I sat on the packed floor, next to Grandad's chair. His knee touched my shoulder every few seconds. In it the monk said, 'The Buddha says that greed is one of the three poisons in our body. You need to decide how much is enough. Too much greed means risk to your peace.'

My grandad had whispered, 'Your dad needs to hear this.'

Was I being greedy, or maximising opportunities for the company and me?

Emily shakes me from my daydreaming. She sits in the chair opposite me. 'Aman, I'd like to take time off. I am mega stressed. My son is going through emotional turmoil for his GCSEs. I will use up the rest of my holidays plus unpaid leave for the next few weeks.'

I don't like Emily not being around. More than managing all the work processes, she balances my negative emotions. She puts her fist under her chin. She waits for me to say 'Yes.'

I know Peter will ask me to take on Tina to join our team temporarily. A few months ago, Tina came up with a brilliant idea she called *time slice,* by lending our digital art only for a short period, resulting in a nice wodge of revenue. I admire Tina for her dedication and achievements. My jealousy stops me from saying this publicly.

Anyway, I don't want anyone disturbing my plans. Tina will find some weaknesses in our approach and will not shy away from telling me.

***

Mona returns with the kids on Sunday afternoon. The wrinkle lines around her eyes have almost disappeared. She gives me a long hug. Nadia gives me a high five and Nabin a tap on my shoulder. They recount the three places they went out to eat and the swimming pool they were allowed to jump into. And the fact that Mona's mum is a genius at the chessboard.

Now, Mona and I are alone in the kitchen. She is scrolling through her phone.

'I got the pictures you sent me from the National Gallery. Looks like you enjoyed the visit. I don't think I have seen that picture of *Holbeen* before.'

She shows me the photo of the painting and says, 'Maybe we can all go there one day.'

I shake my head and laugh. I pronounce *Holbein*. Mona puts her phone down.

She says, 'Mum was asking about you.'

My face must look blank. I can see the slight shake of her head.

She continues, 'I thought you'd want to know that she has recovered from her minor op and is walking much better.' She pauses. I say nothing. She pushes her phone away. 'Mum did say you haven't called her in over six months.'

When we met, I used to spend a lot of time with her at Mona's house. Mona's mum was shorter than her but larger than life. Even before Mona and I got engaged, she talked to me like she had known me her whole life. On my second visit, she made decent *tarkārī*, just using a recipe. She displayed it on the table along with fine cutlery.

It tasted good, but not as good as my mum's, although I refreshed my bowl three times.

I push my chair back. It makes a screeching noise. I walk to the fridge and rearrange the magnets on it.

Mona continues, 'She said she missed hearing your voice. She told me she sometimes worries about you.'

I open the fridge, wanting to disappear inside it. I say, 'I'll call her next week.'

I take out the last can of Coke in the four-piece cardboard packaging and close the door. I move the magnet that is in the shape of a plane to the top of the fridge and into a crash position.

A week later, my worries about Tina are proven correct.

At the team meeting she says, stretching out each syllable, 'I had a look at the risk profiling.' She looks at me like I am twelve years old. 'I think we are not going into the details in the most thorough way we can.' She looks at me again, as if I have created the risk. 'The impact of this is huge, even if the chances of it happening are unlikely. We need to manage the risk of a credit crunch in China and think about what might be in the next wave of fashion that may threaten us.'

***

A month later, I look out of the office window. It's 11 a.m. Ever since the day I joined, Peter's black Ferrari Spider has always been parked in the reserved spot no matter the time. It wasn't there yesterday or today. George fills me in. The fit and healthy Peter, who has run three marathons, is ill. His diary says *On leave*.

He doesn't answer my messages, but ten days later his Ferrari is back.

We meet the day after his return. He looks the same, assured and aloof. 'How's the family, Aman?'

It's the first time Peter has asked in a genuine tone. 'You have two sons, right?'

I correct him and add some non-revealing facts about Nadia and Nabin.

I know nothing about Peter's family. George has insinuated that he has a disabled child, but I have never asked. Raff once said, 'Listen, I know you have so much admiration for Peter. But he is not Superman. Many people have long periods of success before failure strikes. He is vulnerable like everyone else. He will have his own problems in life.'

Peter opens his iPad to go through the statistics. 'I know you've been working long hours on the South American deal. Hope you're balancing work okay with your … domestics. Sorry I mean your home life.'

I am glad Peter has worked out that the word *domestics* is so insensitive.

That evening, I get a ping on my phone. It's from Nadia: *Have you left to come home? We are going to start dinner without you in about thirty minutes. PS. Mum is quite upset with you. She says you sat at the dinner table just twice last week.*

A minute later, I get another text: *Can you take me to the karate class next Thursday, dad? My friend isn't going, so can't grab a lift off her dad.*

I text back: *I can't do it, sorry Nadia, I have a lot of important work to complete.*

Her response has a 😣 on it.

My call with Brazil is next Thursday at 8 p.m., the worst time possible. I need to strike the deal. What excuse can I make to move our meeting? The old lady's words come back to me: *Think of taking advantage of conflict.*

I send a WhatsApp message to Pedro: *Do you mind if we do the video call from my car, as I have to take my daughter to a karate class?*

He replies within two minutes: *Of course. I must also drop my son for his Capoeira class before 6 p.m., here in Sao Paulo, so I will do the same.*

I nod to myself like I know what he is talking about. Afterwards I find a video of Capoeira on Instagram.

A week later, Nadia has a smile of satisfaction. She gets more animated the closer we get to the karate hall. I used to take her to swimming lessons on Thursday at 6:30 p.m., leaving work early. That's when she was three ... I never once let her down.

Pedro connects on Zoom video at 8:02 p.m. I raise my car window.

The first thing he says is, 'So, my friend, tell me more about your daughter's class.'

I tell him about Nadia's style of karate.

He leans forward almost touching the screen. 'Okay, okay, I get it, actually my son does a combination of martial art and movement.' His voice is now excited.

He shares his screen with me and shows me about a dozen pictures of children in dance poses in a traditional white *ghī*. The venue is outdoor by a beach. The Portuguese writing on the lamp-post gives away its location.

I say, 'It's your form of self-expression and cultural identity.'

He laughs like he knows I am reading this off my AI app.

His voice rises and falls like musical notes. I expected a tough negotiation, but we are more like dance partners than shrewd businessmen.

Pedro concludes, 'I look forward to your visit, Aman, to our heritage festival. God willing, I will take you to my son's Capoeira class when you come.'

Two weeks later my sister rings. It's gone past midnight in Mauritius. I keep my video switched off. She keeps hers on.

Her voice is cold. 'How are you, Aman? Hope Mona and the kids are good?'

She doesn't wait for an answer.

'Kaya says you have done virtually nothing for the wedding. A long list of venues is not good enough. You need to go and visit them, arrange the catering and, most importantly, book the *bajrachārya* to conduct the wedding. You remember, for my wedding, we couldn't get a booking with the *bajrachārya* for six months.'

She pauses and looks down, then she says, 'I am as busy as you, but if I need to, I will come to the UK. You told me all was well on our last call. And now you are trying to talk Lekh out of wanting to help. Kaya is so upset.' Her voice rises, 'What is the matter with you?' She breathes heavily. Then, her voice goes quieter. 'I know your friend passed away, and that is very sad.' Her voice rises again, '... but you seem to have time to win big business deals.'

My mum must have relayed my work successes to her. I know they chat several times a week.

She puts her head in her hands and says, 'Kaya is sooooo ... upset.'

I can hear a sob beating into my headpiece. She switches off her video and then cuts off the call.

Two years ago, she wanted to move to Mauritius for a big opportunity. We had a family meeting, and she asked me to keep an eye on Kaya and support our mother. To be fair she offered not to go. 'I don't want to burden you with everything,' she said. I had replied, 'Go for it. That's what Dad would have wanted. I promise you I will take care of Kaya.' I had spent ten minutes boasting that hard work and being a family man were not contradictory.

***

Next Wednesday there is a voice message from Kaya. 'I am passing by, can I pop around at about 9 p.m.? I have invited Uncle Lekh around. I hope you don't mind. Mum said it would be good for Uncle Lekh to help with the wedding planning.'

I can hardly say no.

At 9:05 p.m., there is a knock on the door. Lekh and Kaya both enter together. Did they come in the same car? Have they been talking behind my back? I look outside. Lekh's Toyota is parked on my driveway and Kaya's Volkswagen is on the road.

Lekh holds out his hand. I give him a quick handshake. He hugs Mona like they are long-lost friends. I look at the clock and point them all to the living room.

I start by saying, 'The main thing we are focused on now is finding a venue. We have already shortlisted three halls. Kaya and I will visit them next week to make the booking. The invites are in hand. Once that's done, we can arrange the caterers and the *bajrachāryas*.'

Kaya's pupils move towards Lekh. She says, 'Uncle Lekh said that we need to look at everything together and think about the wedding style first. Didn't you?'

Lekh nods as if on cue. He says, 'We need to think about the theme of the wedding first before considering venues.'

He avoids my eyes. It triggers me. I can feel extra saliva in my mouth. He had avoided eye contact when he refused to lend me money for my MBA.

I stare at him and say, 'Our focus should be on the venue first.'

His head is up but now looking at Kaya.

I say, 'One thing my expensive MBA taught me is to focus on the most important task first.' Why did I mention the MBA? I wish I could rewind.

Lekh closes his eyes.

I want to put my head in my hands. I turn my feet and shoulders towards Kaya. 'Once the venue is done, we can look at everything else.' I spell out details of the Rayish venue on top of our list, highlighting the advantages and disadvantages of the place.

Thirty minutes later, Lekh gets up. He wanders to the clay cup on the mantelpiece and looks inside as if expecting to find Grandad's alcohol. He looks at Kaya and then Mona and smiles at them as if they are teammates. I can feel the back of my teeth clench. Lekh says, 'I need to head back now. It's a good hour drive back.'

I follow him. He puts on his left shoe by the front door.

He looks up and says, 'I'm not sure why you invited me since it seems like you only want to do things your way. I want Kaya's wedding to be a success as much as you do. For the family. But we need to work together and consider different viewpoints.'

He glances at the slightly ajar lounge door and says, 'Not all of us need to follow your vision of things.'

I close the living room door.

He double ties the knot on his left shoe. He says, staring at his shoe, 'I am not sure why you brought up the topic of your MBA. You decided to get a large mortgage, not me. Why would you expect me to sacrifice my family savings to help support your career? And it had nothing to do with our fathers' dispute.'

His right shoe is on much quicker and he is upright now. He raises his voice and looks at me. 'I called three times to arrange for a social after your outburst. I didn't want us to lose our relationship, but you didn't reply. It's you who didn't want to engage, neither then, nor now.'

My upper tummy hurts. Like someone has punched it. I want to hug him and say sorry. But I say, 'Okay, okay, I shouldn't have mentioned the MBA. At the next meeting, we will work together on everything. For family's sake.'

He nods and walks out into the twilight. He doesn't look back.

A week later I have a meeting with Peter to go through contracts. Peter has told me by email that Tina is now permanent in my team. It's noon and I still have some reservoirs of energy. Tina is in his office when I enter. She has her iPad in one hand, and I can see a marked-up document full of fluorescent digital blue marks on it. I turn my body towards Peter and go through the pipeline of work sold. Peter stops me four times and asks for details. Tina nods her head in sync with each of his questions. My throat is parched with talking.

At our last quarter review, Peter kept nodding through my numbers. At that time, he had a big smile, using his calculator app to add numbers on possible contracts. Now it feels like I am in an interrogation cell trapped between a detective and a torturer. I want Peter to congratulate me on numbers 19% higher than last quarter. I am hot now and my throat is dry. As soon as the meeting finishes, I get up fast. I knock my phone, and it goes under the table. My stomach releases as I bend down. The trouser button pops out and lands on top of the phone screen. Tina has a clear view of the button. Her mouth is closed, but her tummy is moving with laughter. Worse than that, the zip is not staying in place.

I head to the water fountain and gulp as much as I can. I press the lift button. When the door opens there are five people all looking at me. I turn around and walk down the five floors of stairs to the car park. My rain jacket in the boot is scrunched up in a large black ball. The sun is shining with two small clouds in the sky. The bottom of the jacket reaches the top of my thighs, covering up most of my embarrassment. Almost everyone walking past me is solo, bar one mother with a pram. Not one person glances at my black jacket; all are either talking on a phone or walking fast to their destination. I head to the second-floor clothing department of M&S. It's a place

I have not been to before. I touch the bluish-green colour trousers. It reminds me of the backdrop of greenery in Botticelli's paintings.

The children's section adjoins the gents' section. A young girl, she must be around four years old, is out with her grandmother. Their movements are all so slow and they seem to be doing more talking than examining things.

I have two pairs of grey trousers in hand and pass the grandmother on the way to the changing room.

She asks, 'Why do you like blue, Natalie?'

The little girl replies, 'Because it's the colour of my horse, Cha Cha.'

I can't remember seeing a child under five in the last two years. I hardly went shopping with Nadia or Nabin. It was all left to Mona.

The second set of trousers I try are more comfortable, but they are size 40, the largest I have worn in my life. I walk past them again, wearing the grey trousers with the tag in my hand. They haven't moved.

The girl points up. 'Grandad told me the colour blue is after the word sky; it's my favourite colour.'

Neither of them is looking at a single piece of merchandise. It's all so slow. I have an urge to ask them to hurry up and choose something. When I get to the checkout, there is a queue of six. I check the time on my watch twice. My next meeting is in seventeen minutes. I turn around to see the grandmother and child, fifty metres away and still engaged in a conversation. There is still not a single item in their wire basket.

Ten minutes later, I pay up. I turn my head at the top of the escalator. Both are laughing and waving their hands. I'd swap myself to be either one of them right now. My grandad used to take me on walks in Bushey market. We bought a Batman T-shirt, but only after we spent almost an hour bartering at different stalls. Grandad knew many of the stallholders by name.

Nowadays, I am a frequent flyer to the vending machine on the second floor. It is also where one of our IT suppliers, or 'technology partners' as they call themselves, is located. The machine is my friend and I know the numbers for sea salt crisps (D7) and mint creams (E4) by heart. Yesterday, I peeked into the open-plan office after I got my snack. I saw Louis chatting animatedly with two techies. He was more upright and more confident than when he is on the fourth floor. There is an astringent smell, and I can hear the mainframe humming in the background. They are all standing up. So, this is where Louis does all his wheeling to get around technical issues. All around the room, everyone is staring at computer screens. Half are in T-shirts and the others in unironed, cheap, short-sleeved shirts. I am glad I don't work here.

In Friday's board meeting, I am given my twenty-minute slot. I read through the bullet points on our deals with Chinese distributors. I say, 'It's unlikely the rise of the rich will stop, particularly in Asia.'

The non-executive director, Hardeep, is making notes on her device as I speak. She is wearing one piece of jewellery, a bright silver bangle on her right wrist. Her back goes erect just as I finish. Peter is looking at her. His brow is furrowed. I spotted the two of them talking outside Peter's office yesterday. They had stepped into the meeting room as soon as they saw me.

She says, 'Aman, you must have seen the recent news. Why do you think we won't be impacted by the crunch?' She swipes her device and says, 'I must say, I found Tina's reports very compelling about the high risk we are taking on.' She looks at the gold at the top of my right wrist.

I put up my research slide, pointing my hand to the bullet points. 'The market thinks that impact to the affluent will be limited from any shock.'

She stops twisting the bangle on her wrist. The script form is the same as used in Nepal, but I think the language is Hindi.

Peter interrupts my following sentence. He says, 'We are working on ensuring we have an improved risk process in place. Aman will report back with an update at the next meeting.'

She stops the twisting of the bangle. I keep a straight face but want to sigh out loud.

The Chair moves onto the next item and I sit back. I pretend to listen by nodding and writing on my iPad. But I want to run away from the woman two seats to my right.

The Chair takes me to one side at the interval. I can feel my breath – it's heavy. He smiles at me, 'Aman, it's incredible what you have developed in the last three months. Your value to DigiArt is well regarded. Peter has great trust in you. I am so glad the board has taken a majority view to push ahead with your area of product development.' His smile is almost a laugh. 'Hardeep does ask difficult questions. You'll get used to her. Well, do keep an eye on risk.'

I give him the most confident response I can manage. I am not sure I am enjoying this role anymore. I don't enjoy all the questioning. No-one challenged me much on the third or fourth floor.

***

A few days later, my life changes forever. Our agent based in Shanghai doesn't respond to my emails. I get a terse letter from a Chinese customer saying, *Please stop chasing us for payment. We already paid via your agent a month ago.* I call the agent and get a dead tone. And their website has disappeared. There is an intense pain on the left side of my chest. I call the number another six times, the gaps in between getting shorter. I give up after two long hours.

I find the finance team on the third floor, all looking stern. We go over the trail of documents as if we are fitting together a puzzle.

As we check the banking documents, it hits me. In my focus to sign off the Brazil deal I hadn't checked the bank details in the contract for our Shanghai customer. Someone from the agent had amended our bank account and replaced it with an offshore bank. If Emily was around, she would have checked routinely on my behalf. On the steps back up, I thump my fist against the wall. Please let something correct this ... an email or a phone call to explain the mistake. I am like a tyre with no air. I can't think of any legitimate excuse to give to Peter. It was my responsibility to do all the final checks on the contract.

There is no-one I can blame.

That afternoon, I sit in Peter's office. He listens without any response as I deliver the facts within my grasp. The CEO joins us a few minutes later. I repeat everything again, this time in a different order. The CEO's face has no expression, but his black eyes are as still as a deep dark lake. He nods once I finish. I expected an interrogation. I am shivering when I return to my desk. On my laptop wallpaper is the background picture of a Himalayan mountain – sent from one of my cousins in Nepal. I see myself on the very edge of one of the cliffs.

That evening, the churning in my mind gets worse. I sit on my bed, draw the curtains and keep the bedroom door closed. That agent in China wanted to rush decisions. I had not done enough checks. I start searching on the net. The agent already has a civil case against it. They have three adverse credit reports all dated in the last six months.

I have had fraud training twice during the last six years. This scam was on my watch. It's obvious. My drive to forge relationships and work at speed had created my blind spot. They had taken the money from our customers as part of a planned move and disappeared. Trying to work with the Chinese authorities to get the money back would be impossible.

The pain in my chest is permanent, I can't make it go away. I go over all the facts in my mind again and again.

Over the next few days, I ignore my family. If anything, I grunt out mumbles. The first out of the kitchen after dinner. Mona spends all her evenings in the living room with the kids. All my time is spent on myself, my mistake and my career. At work, I spend energy trying to find a way to find our money via bank tracing but get nowhere. I daydream about some magical email from the agent saying, *We have made a mistake please accept our apologies and the full transfer of money to DigiArt.* The email will never materialise. Raff comes up in my thoughts as if he is alive. He would have listened to my explanations. Then said something cryptic that would have calmed me.

Things get worse. Two weeks later, there is a stock market drop of 9% in China and there is talk of one of their banks being insolvent. The next day there's a further drop of 7% and Tina puts all our Chinese contracts on the corporate high-risk register.

The next day, without warning, the Chinese government put in foreign exchange controls. The controls are on non-basic goods and services. I realise this means we can't export our art to them.

That afternoon, I skip lunch. I head to the park. I need to speak to the old lady. I look around in a zigzag motion, trying to spot her. Maybe she can understand my garbled mind and my burden. I sit on one end of the nearest empty bench. My left hand is on my forehead and my gaze is on my feet. The sun is hot and I am sweating heavily. I want to call my mum but put the phone back in my pocket. She will give a shoulder to cry on and sympathy. What I want is someone who will understand.

Like Raff.

The bench vibrates. The old lady is sitting at the opposite end. She wears a different coat; it's cream and thin.

She points to the grass on our left. 'The pigeons seem to return here. It's interesting why they do. They say that pigeons have a sharp memory for such a small brain.'

She chuckles and moves her hand towards her mouth. She gazes into my face; her laugh wanes and eyes look concerned.

I want to spill the beans and tell her everything about Raff, my job, my problems at home, but I don't know how to start.

'Can I ask you,' I say, 'what do you think about society today? Is it going in the right direction?'

She plays along. 'Well, people asked the same question in the 70s as well. You should see the change we had then. It's down to us to decide how to adapt in today's society and what to move away from. We have to flow with a fast-moving river but can still decide on which fork to take.'

I have a clear picture of the Bagmati River, the sole rapid river I have ever seen. That was when I visited Kathmandu. I see myself swimming against the tide, looking for a fork out.

She taps her stick against the bench. She says, 'After your advice, I invested in nano broadband and now I see both my grandkids crystal clear every day! I can even make out the muck on their school uniform! It's a shame as I live just three miles away from them. I wish they would visit me after school but this is better than swimming against the tide.'

I say, 'Yes, but the river tide is carried by status, selfishness and success. It's overpowering, don't you think?'

She says nothing for thirty seconds. My knees are clapping together. Then she says, 'Status and success are not bad things at all, I am not one for timidity.'

I want her to say something else, like *Quit your job and become a monk*. My thighs start squeezing into the bench.

'You are like my daughter. She likes success and status. I don't have a problem with that.' She laughs and looks into the sky. 'But I did tell her once that she needs to have some inner aspirations as well.'

Her mouth widens. Perhaps to say more about her daughter. But she closes it. She reaches for her stick and looks at her watch. I gaze at her face with more attention. I can see beyond the wrinkles and full set of grey hair. The high cheekbones and the alert eyes. Her back is bent but her shoulders are straight.

The next day I get a diary request to join the CEO and Peter for a meeting. It's with thirty minutes' notice. I prepare as much as I can, guessing what questions are coming. But I am in trouble. It's like Kaya's knock on the door a few weeks ago, but much worse.

Both the CEO and Peter have eyes that have softened from the last time I met them. They sit in tandem next to each other. Their arms unfolded. One has a light blue shirt and the other crème white. They are both without a wrinkle. Each with an identical device in their hand. They could be two brothers. Between them is a brown envelope. It's quite thin. There can't be much inside. My breath goes out. Some decision has been made.

The CEO says, 'Aman, the current events are a concern, but it doesn't take away from the incredible work you've done over the last two years. In particular, in this new role. Everyone is in awe of your determination and stakeholder skills.'

This is all dressing up; I know the bad news is coming.

He pauses. There is a lump in my throat. My arms fold together.

His voice is soft. 'We are not convinced the board will be satisfied with your explanation on risk and the pace you went at. Hardeep will want some resolution, probably a scalp. You will have to be it.'

Peter glances at his device and then on the wall to my right.

I manage to get some air in my thudding chest. I want to jump from the window opposite.

The CEO continues, 'You know how keen the board is on our reputation as a company. They see risk and opportunity in equal measure. I think we can all agree, the lack of due diligence on that agent. We now know the risk of a credit crunch, which was much higher than you alluded to at the last board meeting. We have already lost prime customers, and the pipeline is getting dry.'

Why doesn't he just say I messed up and stop repeating what I know?

I look at the door on my left. I want to burst through it and run down the five floors to my car. But my feet seem as if they are stuck to the floor.

'I am afraid you will have to lie low for a while.' He looks at Peter like they are in a band. The CEO clears his throat. He says, 'We don't want to terminate your employment, Aman.'

I was waiting for the word *sack*, but *terminate* sounds much worse. The CEO's gaze is unwavering. He taps the table.

'Actually, Peter and I have an offer for you. Our partner on the second floor has an IT infrastructure management role that needs filling. I have already spoken to them, and they would welcome your skills. You have a good relationship with them already, Aman. Your expertise means that you can make some improvements to their processes.'

I want to say, *I hardly go to the second floor.* Instead I blurt out, 'Who will do my job?'

The CEO looks at Peter. Peter puts his device down.

He says in a wavering voice, 'We are going to move Tina to look after your New Products team.'

The CEO's voice has a hint of kindness. 'Another opportunity will come, Aman. You have to be patient and spend some time reflecting.'

He pauses, waiting for me to absorb. The CEO's eyes are unmoved.

I have an instant image of the film *Jaws*. My dad took me to see a re-release in the 90s. I am being ripped up and eaten alive and my legs are halfway inside the shark's mouth.

My mouth blurts out, 'What option do I have?'

I look at Peter. He looks at the CEO. The CEO's answer sounds like a recorded message. 'Well, you can try your hand at the job market. But you may have trouble with references.'

Then he blinks three times, like Lekh does. It's the first time I have noticed him do this.

He says, 'It's entirely up to you, I know you have mouths to feed like the rest of us.'

Peter chips in, 'I think the best option is to take the new role.'

Out of the shark's mouth appears a montage of objects. My credit cards, a piece of paper with the words *mortgage costs* and my replica Renaissance painting torn in pieces. I realise that I won't make the trip to Rio.

He pushes the paperwork in my direction slowly, but I can hear the skids from the pressure; the envelope is upside down with the flap unsealed. On the bottom of the first page, I find the number. The pay is a drop of 30%. This is the same room where I got my two promotions on the same headed notepaper. I look up and see four eyes on me like I have been reduced to some sort of beggar.

Afterwards, Peter ushers me to his office. He starts playing with his Montblanc pen.

He says, 'Just work on the second floor for a little while. Who knows what opportunities will arise again. The company is just going through a blip, and you've been caught in the firing line.'

Both my fists are clenched and on top of the table. My gut says getting another job will take months. My competition will be the new generation of twenty-year-olds working in Cloud technology.

He looks at my face and shakes his head. 'Don't take it so personally. I know you've worked extremely hard, but shit happens.'

I like the word *shit,* at least it's more direct.

I say, 'You backed me, Peter, with what I was doing. Now you have hung me out to dry – all in front of the CEO. You know the hours and thought I've put in.' My open hand is holding my chin up.

Peter says nothing. He moves his pen in a clockwise direction around his thumb. I forget what I say next. That's normal when I get upset. What I do know is I say a lot. When I get up, Peter's right hand is trembling. His pen is resting on the table. He's looking towards the ceiling. I want to punch his office door open. Very hard.

I head straight home. I have the radio on. The news summary is about some earthquake in Turkey. Whenever there is some natural disaster far away, I am grateful that my family is not caught up in it. Today, it's white noise in the background. They are interviewing locals. I can feel the misery in their voices. I leave the radio on; much better to hear the sound of suffering people than my own thoughts.

Once home, I head straight to my room, lock the door and jump on the bed. My shoes are still on. The letter of change of role is cold. My desk is down two floors and right next to the noisy IT machinery room. I shudder. I will be managing four IT staff and improving infrastructure processes. Boredom will be my torture. There are two small tears in my eyes and the lump in my throat is back. I always have bits of conversation at the dinner table about my work. What am I going to talk to the kids about every evening? The sole good thing is that the vending machine is on the same floor. I want to tear the letter but instead I put it under my pillow.

There is a shout from downstairs, 'Come down for dinner, Dad!'

I drag the chair to the kitchen table, which makes a loud noise. I can't keep it in for any longer. All three members of the family turn their heads. I stumble over my words, blurting out everything, mixing up bits. My thoughts are a jumbled mess, mixing up the events of my future, the mistake I made and the demotion that came today. I take a deep breath and try to give more structure to what I am saying. But I just speak faster.

Mona sits next to me. She gives me a glass of water.

Nabin says, 'Dad, it's a job, who cares what floor you work on. I don't.'

'Sounds like you will be home every day by 6 p.m.,' says Mona.

Both my kids' eyes light up, their faces breaking into broad smiles. Mona puts *kākrō ko achār* on my plate – the cucumber is finely cut, like it has gone through a shredder, coated in mustard.

I get another five minutes of sympathy and that lifts me – at least for now.

Then Nabin says, 'The coach of the Saturday club is leaving and no-one knows who is taking over. I hope Uncle Kishan steps forward, he would make a good coach.'

I have my first mouthful of the mushroom pie. I am playing with the rest of it with my fork.

Nadia says, 'Mum and I made the pastry from scratch. Don't you think it tastes amazing?'

It tastes of rubber to me.

I don't want to be in the bedroom. And I don't want to be with anyone. I find my toolbox in the garage and start working on the broken chair. It's close to dusk but the low lighting of the garage doesn't bother me.

My golf bag is on the left, untouched for four months. As I chisel out the broken piece from the chair, I start writing out my resignation letter in my mind. I sigh; I want to head off to Raff's house. He would have sat me down in his conservatory and understood everything.

He would have given me hope, shown me a way.

Mona finds me an hour later. I am sitting on the toolbox sanding down the joint, trying to make the wood grain finer and finer.

'What are you planning to do, Aman?' she says.

I stand up and rummage for wood glue. 'No idea,' I reply.

She remains by the open door. The breeze is cooler now, and she follows my hands with her gaze.

I hear my words coming out spontaneously, 'I cannot risk redundancy, it may take time to get a role and anyway the location could be all wrong. The days of working from home have gone, so not much chance of that either.'

Applying for jobs while mulling in the house scares me. Each rejection email would be like a little dagger into my heart. I need to get out of the house. I sit back down on the toolbox and look at the floor. Mona moves next to me, takes my hand, touches my wrist and starts counting. She has no medical qualification, yet she has picked up a lot by working in a hospital.

She says, still holding my wrist, 'Your pulse is so high, almost 120. You told me at your last check-up that all was well?'

I pick up the chisel and search for burrs on the joint.

I was offered a place on a stress reduction clinic from the GP. I had ignored the reminder. 'I'll book a GP appointment next week.'

Mona steps back three steps. I am staring at the chisel. She is staring at me.

My mindless chiselling takes away too much wood. I shout, 'That's the problem.'

Mona jolts backwards.

'That's the problem. I don't know what I want.' I drop the chisel on the floor, leave the chair upside down and put my head in my hands as Mona puts her hand on my shoulder.

At work the next day, I feel like an animal in the zoo who is being watched. No-one comes close. I rely on autopilot in responding to emails and completing administrative tasks. At 10 a.m., I have an urge to get out of the building. It's already a warm day. Nowadays I avoid the lift. I walk as fast as possible down the four floors. Strangely, my ears pop when I reach the bottom. As I wait at the pedestrian crossing, a huge truck comes my way with the words *Office Supplies* all over it. I'm on the edge of the pavement, the top of my shoes over it. Jumping in front of the truck seems more than appealing. All pain would disappear. There is a fair chance that my next life could be better. And the company life insurance would protect the family. The driver hoots full blast as he goes past. His mate winds down the passenger window, looks at me while turning his index finger around the side of his head. He shouts, 'Crazy man!' I wonder how many ways there are to commit suicide. I almost want to ask my AI app, but they are programmed never to provide that information. I shake my head and start grinning. I have no idea where the thought came from – it's completely unlike me.

I keep walking and get to the park entrance. I want to find the old lady, but I also don't want her to see me as I am now. I turn back and end up at the coffee shop. The blonde lady, whose name I now know is Annetta, exchanges pleasantries as she scans my app. My words are all fake. She looks at my Rolex watch and then my golden bracelet.

She says, 'No work meeting here today?'

I shrug and sit in the furthest place from the front door. There are two other people nearby on individual tables, their fingers moving in a rhythm on the keyboards of their laptops.

My hands add three sachets of brown sugar one by one into the coffee as I stir. It makes the white swirl in the middle of the large cup turn clockwise.

'Oh, hello.'

My neck twists to the left. It clicks twice. The old lady from the park is waving. Next to her is a boy around six years old. I assume he must be her grandson. I nod to the seat in front of me. She waves her stick at Annetta, as she brings her tray and puts it next to mine. The boy sits close to me, as if I am his own dad. He is eyeing the sugar sachets. The old lady sets down her green purse and moves the two cups onto the table. She gives a napkin and the hot chocolate to the boy.

Like a tidal wave, I blurt out, 'I've been kind of sacked and will work on the second floor.'

'Ohh,' she says, her eyelids open wider. She stirs her drink, encouraging the boy to drink slowly. She chuckles as he gulps down a mouthful. 'I got demoted in '81 for answering back to my boss and got moved to the basement. The funny thing was, I became his boss three years later in '84.'

She stirs her cup more. I don't remember her adding any sugar. She closes her eyes briefly.

'It was a wonderful opportunity to lie low and have time to reflect. Plus, of course it allowed me time to join the fencing club where I met my husband.'

Her grandson now has smudges of hot chocolate around his mouth and nose. His feet are paddling underneath the table.

She continues, 'People talk about how things change fast nowadays, but even in my day there was plenty of change about! Jobs weren't as pleasant as some people make out. Perhaps you should see this as an opportunity and not a setback, and I bet you my boss was worse than yours.'

I put my head in my hands. I only did that at home and with Raff. The little boy taps my elbow twice. I lift my head and he flashes his teeth. He starts talking to the old lady about his toys at home. I lean back and observe their to-ing and fro-ing. Five minutes later, there is a bleep from the old lady's purse. She tuts and gets up. The six-year-old gives me a fist bump on the way out. He reminds me of a young Nabin; his eyes were always wide whenever I made him hot chocolate. Annetta gives me a smile and then a wave on my way out. I feel a tiny flame of light in the middle of my chest.

As soon as I get back to the office, any inner light within me dies. It's triggered with the receptionist ignoring me at the automated gates. She usually mentions something mundane. But I can sense her eyes following me as I open the stairwell door. I have a peek at the second-floor office rooms on my way up. It has the faint smell of metal and a gentle 'whirrrr' from the computer room. The light seems to be fainter than the fourth even with the same arrangement of windows and fluorescent tubes. From the corner of my eye the Head of Technology walks in my direction. I move back to the vending machine by the lift, press D7 and wait for the salted crisp packet to fall out.

I am an impostor in my own team. Tina sits twenty feet away and avoids all conversation with me. Yet she sends me plenty of emails, asking me for the whereabouts of a file or something about processes. Nobody ever seems to be in the kitchenette with me at the same time. My chest has an inward pain, as if someone is pressing from the top. Emily would understand and give me some support. I want to reach out to her but don't have the courage. That would also be a sign of complete weakness.

That afternoon, to make matters worse, George cracks more jokes than usual with the rest of the team. I don't even bother trying to make sense of his punch lines. I plough through my work, giving it enough attention not to be shoddy, but without any care. I wish I could leave early today, but there are many loose ends to complete.

Late in the afternoon, there is a clink sound. The roller chairs are moving. The clock says 6:05 p.m. The cleaner is here. Early. If I am working late, she usually comes over. She knows I run this team. The topic is either about the state of the kitchenette on the second floor or a moan about travel delays. But today she ignores me as she sweeps the wooden floor. She wouldn't know about my status, would she? She gets closer to my desk.

She says with a worried face, 'How are you, sir? You look so busy, so I didn't want to disturb you.' She looks at me and says, 'You look troubled.'

She turns up the vacuum cleaner speed before I can defend myself and moves away.

George gives me a slap on the back. He has his Primark jacket in his hand. We are the last two people left in the office.

'Cheer up geezer.'

He whistles an upbeat tune all the way to the lift. I can't hold it in, I have hate for everyone in this office, particularly George.

CHAPTER 6

GOING NOWHERE

Saturday takes ages to arrive. It's the first day of the pre-season training, and I am feeling a flame of excitement about taking Nabin to football. This time last year, we were discussing who bought who in the Premier League, or I would be explaining something technical. This year, Nabin says nothing. Well – he mumbles to my prompts. I have been warned by Emily about the onset signs of teen-agehood in boys. I want the feeling of connection back.

We stop when I hear an ambulance siren, but it fades away. Nabin continues to fiddle with his phone. We used to improvise any conver-sation and always found something to giggle about. Once, when he was eight, we passed an emergency ambulance coming in the opposite direction. We had invented a whole new world about the sound it made and how to adapt it for different emergencies. A higher pitched wailing noise would mean 'going to a car accident,' and a lower pitched wailing noise would mean a 'football accident.'

As I park, he utters just one proper sentence: 'Kishan has agreed to be our new coach next season.'

I say to him, 'Uncle Kishan to you.'

Kishan told me once, 'You are proper old school, Aman. I love being called Uncle. Nobody uses that term anymore unless you are the real deal.'

On the field, Kishan is setting up. I help him put up the goal.

I say, 'Everyone says you will make a great coach this season.'

He shrugs like he's been doing it for years. He waves his phone at me. 'Look at this. We have booked a trip to the Peak District,' he says. 'Got a mega deal by searching online, a seven-night holiday for £490 for a two-bedroom in Ashbourne.'

He looks at me and says, 'You been there?'

I shake my head. The £490 is only 5% of the Egypt holiday, which is the next destination on my plan.

'What's more, one of our care homes is there and the manager is going to take us on a countryside walk around a big hill. There is also Chatsworth House. Maybe you'd like that? You like the old-worldly stuff, don't you?'

I shrug my shoulders.

'Anyway, when is your trip to Egypt?' Before I can reply, he heads off to meet the growing number of parents and kids.

I don't even know where the Peak District is. Is it somewhere in the middle of England? I have hardly been anywhere outside of twenty miles of my house in the UK. I have only ever been twice to Brighton and a weekend in Bath. I knew the layout of Heathrow terminals better than the map of England. A holiday to me always meant finding a beautiful hotel in an exotic land. I thrived on showing the pictures to whoever I could impress.

The Egypt trip includes two excursions and a visit to the Valley of the Kings. I want to see the carvings there. The holiday brochure said the mathematical and geometric principles used in ancient Egypt were also in Renaissance art.

That evening, I check three travel sites. I can get 10% off if I book by the end of the month. I open the front cover of my book by my bedside table. It arrived three weeks ago.

The title is *Connecting Ancient Egypt with the Renaissance*.

At 11 p.m., there is a beep on the phone, while I am scrolling through Instagram's Egypt tag. *Uncle Aman, I need your help … can I call you next week one morning? Thank you! Kaya* ☺. I want to call Kaya now. Instead, I reply: *Call me anytime, earlier if you wish* 👍.

The following Monday I start on the second floor. My manager is five years younger than me. He gave me all the respect I demanded when he was my supplier. Now, he shows me the list of regular tasks and meetings. His words are polite, yet clear, but I know who is in charge. The work is easy enough. My biggest dread is bumping into my team or the directors in the common lift. I use the stairs as much as possible. Gossip travels fast. My goal is to exit or enter the building without talking to the receptionist or security guard.

On my third day in my new job, Kaya rings. Her voice is wavering like the hum of the server room ten metres away.

'You won't believe it. That venue we discussed is no longer available due to some health and safety order.'

She pauses. I say nothing … The noise from the server room's cooling systems hums louder.

'Uncle, I need your help. Can you give me the details of the wedding planner you mentioned before?'

My heart cools, yet the heat in my neck gets higher. 'Kaya, we can do this ourselves, we don't need a planner.'

Her response is instant, like it's prepared. She says, 'That's fine, but I want Uncle Lekh involved with everything from now on.'

As soon as the call ends, I throw my phone onto the desk, and the noise strengthens the hum. The two people facing me don't even look up.

On the second floor, I get into a mechanical habit. For ten days, I go every day to Zeno's for a drink at 10:30 a.m.

My favourite table, on the right of the entrance, away from the windows, is gone if I get there after 11 a.m. There is a big refurbishment project thirty metres from Zeno's. The labourers all have huge hands that make the coffee mugs look tiny. They occupy all the seating space, munching sandwiches. I avoid my usual posh coffee shop altogether, not wanting to bump into anyone from the fourth floor or above. A pity since I liked seeing Annetta – the last time she asked me about the latest in art technology.

Some days later, we have a meeting to look at upgrading our software controls for our R840 servers at 10 a.m. My topmost thought is whether I will get to Zeno's well before 11 a.m. I scan the papers in three minutes, just picking up keywords.

The meeting in the windowless office goes quicker than planned. I keep my contribution to a minimum. A few minutes later, I hold my large mug of instant coffee, sitting at my favourite table. *The Metro* is always on the table, and today, mine has dark smudges of two fingers from a builder's hand on the front page. An article on page three has the title: *30% of Men Have Mental Health Issues at Work*. I search for the exact definition of depression in the Oxford online dictionary. It reads: *Feelings of severe despondency and dejection*. That is exactly me. It is almost 11:15 a.m., the café nearly full.

George's figure is in the corner of my eye. His gait is obvious. A wobble from left to right, with short steps followed by occasional long ones. I pull *The Metro* closer to my face. My neck is locked on the crossword on the corner of page eleven. I look at seven across: *Art's blending with reality creates unity (6)*. I want to melt away. When I look up three minutes later, he is gone.

Every day since I arrived on the second floor, I have two packets of crisps from the vending machine on my return from Zeno's.

Today, the D7 slot for sea salt crisps is completely empty. This stupid machine from the last century keeps running out. It has been happening every Thursday for the last three weeks. I air-kick the base of the machine. I wish Zeno's sold these, but they only do ready salted. My email to the office manager reads: *The vending machine is empty of sea salt crisps (slot D7) late in the week. Can we change the filling dates to twice a week or, better still, have two rows for sea salt crisps? There are two slots for the tortilla crisps (slots A7 and A8). They are unlikely to be in high demand, so one can be used for sea salted crisps. Furthermore, can you fix the contactless payment system? It is not working and the system flashes red. I don't have the habit of carrying money. Anyhow, isn't it inefficient to keep emptying the machine of cash?*

Three weeks ago, I was managing contracts with a total of over a million pounds. I was balancing the supply and demand of our cutting-edge products. Now I am giving advice on the management of the supply and demand of £1.50 crisps. I find the *bcc* button and automatically put Raff's email in. I often copied Raff on work emails – like the ones when I was responding to some conflict, a big success or sometimes something silly. I close my eyes and clench both fists. I delete Raff's name.

The whirr of the computer room grows louder as the morning advances. It's 28°C outside, and the cooling system is on overdrive. I time my lunch break at 12:45 p.m. to avoid the queue for sandwiches. I stop work, even if I am in the middle of something. Raff would have agreed – my job is boring but necessary ... I break the tasks into small, planned chunks on my calendar, which makes it look busy. When it's time to go home, I don't leave at five o'clock sharp; that would mean I am a clock watcher. So, it's always between ten and fifteen minutes past. My colleague has paperwork in all four corners of his desk and two unopened technology magazines in recycled wrapping. The guy opposite has three odd-shaped mugs on his table, a biking magazine, a tub of jellybeans and *The Metro*. He has a 100-gram chocolate wrapper sitting on the biking magazine.

So far, there has been no friction with my manager. I guess Peter must have had a word with him on how to manage me. Once a day, sometimes more, I daydream about getting my job back. In that dream, I imagine Tina turning out to be a failure and getting shown the door. The CEO is begging me in the boardroom, asking me to return. And there is wild spontaneous clapping when I return to the fourth floor. When I get bored, I rework all the reporting charts. I change layouts and chart types and experiment with colours.

Today, I have an urge to browse through the National Gallery's Renaissance paintings on my wide screen. But that is impossible in plain sight of three colleagues.

I have stopped looking at job apps. I have no willpower to attend an interview. Anyway, my LinkedIn profile hasn't been updated and I have no intention to do so. The question of the demotion would come up at my interview. Unless I lied, I would have to explain my failure. I am unemployable.

I am three weeks into my new job and, every evening, I flop into bed as soon as I get home. I am not sleepy but close my eyes anyway and daydream about being on the fourth floor.

There is a knock on the door.

Nabin says from the other side, 'When is dinner?'

My watch says 7:55 p.m. I have been in my room for over ninety minutes. I look out of the bedroom window. Mona's parking spot is empty. My text to her is unanswered. The gas stove has a lentil curry with silver foil covering it. The pot is cold. While I warm the food, I call Mona's phone and get a dead tone.

At 9 p.m., I watch a Sky Arts documentary on the history of painting. I learn that the columns in the background of one of

Botticelli's paintings are influenced by the Egyptian papyrus style. As the credits start, a coldness wells up. I call Mona again, but I get the same status. My fingers fire up Google Maps and I type *traffic incident*. There is a queue mark in red with the word accident and a red car icon at the top of the A4140. All the details from Raff's collision come back to me, but this time I see Mona in the driving seat. She is lying still in a seat, with her seatbelt missing. Her door is completely smashed and open. I call again.

As soon as the big hand of the clock indicates it's past 10:15 p.m., I wait no more. My car keys are in my hand. I yell to the kids 'Popping out,' not waiting for a reply. As I am about to pull out, on my right, I see a bright flash from the headlights of a car in the dark. The car gets closer; the circular lights mean it may be Mona's BMW. The low hum of the electric motor confirms it. My heart pounds even louder. She parks in her slot, blinks and waves to me.

I shout, 'Where the hell have you been?'

She opens her car door. There is movement on my left. My neighbour's first-floor window opens. I can see his head jutting out.

Mona whispers, 'I told you, when I left, we had a leaving do today. Had you forgotten?'

She closes the car door and holds me by my elbow. 'Let's go in and we can talk there.'

As soon as the front door closes, she puts her hand on my shoulder and says, 'I sent you a text, but my phone must have run out of charge. Anyway, there was an accident on the A4140, and you know there is no signal at the top of that hill.'

She opens the kitchen door, and I follow in. She puts some of the lentils in a pot and twists her thumb. The gas flame is full.

She turns around and says, 'You look terrible.'

I throw my keys on the table. 'Sorry to yell, I completely forgot and when I got no answer, well ... Raff came to mind.'

She turns the flame off and takes a plate out for me. My tummy is churning but I have no appetite. Afterwards, we load the dishwasher together, saying nothing. I am both elated and angry at myself.

Mona yawns. 'You look petrified.' She turns around from the dishwasher and says, 'Aman, don't be hard on yourself. I should have called to remind you.'

***

One of our monthly meetings is on the fourth floor with one of the managers at DigiArt. This will be my first visit in almost two months. I am with my manager and have no choice but to use the lift. The lift door opens; Peter's PA is there. She mouths a 'Hello.'

I press my hand hard on the number four and say, 'I have a meeting at eleven on the fourth floor.' I don't know why I have to spell this out.

She says nothing. She gazes at my chest and has a smirk. She pushes the fifth-floor button. It was already lit. Her eyes gaze up and down my T-shirt for the rest of the journey.

We walk past the large meeting room, the same one where I used to hold my team events. My old team and Tina are there. They are all in a semicircle like they are all united. The whiteboard has several flow charts drawn on it with Tina next to it holding the dark blue colour marker, the one I liked. Everyone has a smile on their face. I walk two steps forward and then back and look through the glass again. Not a single person turns their head in my direction. With or without me, the team relationship and purpose has carried on.

I run out of things to do at about 3 p.m. On many days, I spend fifteen minutes in the bathroom on the ground floor trying to escape the noise. Today, I type *Are there Titian interest groups in London* into my GPT, while sitting on a closed toilet seat in a cubicle. The second line identifies *Titian Followers Group London*, or as they say,

TFG. Their ornate Instagram page has four of his paintings arranged in a square. I shake my head. They meet at 6 p.m. every Thursday, the same evening as Nadia's karate class. I keep asking the GPT. The fourth time round it informs me of the *Botticelli Discussion Group* which meets on Mondays. The venue is eight stations away on the Central line. Their website hasn't been refreshed for many years, and the font is hard to read on my 6-inch phone.

On Monday, I forgo my car and take the tube so that I can attend the Botticelli meet. It's down a narrow side street away from the main roads with the posh buildings of Kensington. The location is the basement of a charity office room, a five-minute walk from the station. I am ten minutes early, but there are seven other people already there. I button my jacket. The AC setting must be set to low. After the third handshake, I stop remembering any names. That happens when I am nervous. Some are tall and some are short, some dressed smart and one person in a track suit, but their conversations are slow and deliberate. I am the youngest one there. Just from the chit-chat, they have more knowledge about paintings than I do, but then I expected that. The basement is not in great condition for office space. Gazing up, I see large stains on the ceiling that look like a water leak. The poster on the wall says, *Aging with Dignity, Housed with Pride*. I figure a homeless charity for older people is based here. The vanilla paint seems to have been there for years, if not decades. It has turned into a weak yellow colour. My windowed, second-floor office is not so bad after all.

Just before we start, two latecomers join. One looks familiar. She is in a business suit. Everyone greets her like she is someone important. I realise it is Joan, the director at ArtCloudo. That's where I sold my first proposal a few months ago. I drift to the corner of the room, diagonally furthest away from Joan. The evening's talk is on Botticelli's later years.

The speaker says, 'Here in this scene, Botticelli paints Zenobius, who walks away from a proposed marriage with a beautiful woman to seek salvation. As we can see, he also gets his mother to convert, before being baptised by the Pope.'

So much like the Buddha who leaves his material life to seek salvation. A story I know well from the many times I attended the *Bāhā* with Grandad. Once I turned sixteen, I was never encouraged to go. My grandad had told my mum once, 'Let Aman decide for himself. The Buddha was against coercion.' Now I wish I had been pushed more – perhaps I could have learnt to let go like the Buddha.

I can see why this style of painting was so popular on our product platforms for reuse. The angular Florentine buildings, based on Roman antiquity, drew you into the scene.

She continues, 'As we can see, in the *Last Miracle* painting, showing Zenobius on his deathbed, it shows his deep love of God and, with it, his unbounded faith.'

She then puts up a picture – a scene of three people brought back to life.

'The panels, particularly of the painting in New York, show how earlier in his life Zenobius restores life due to the faith of miracles and restoration.'

I unbutton my jacket as it gets warmer. I wish someone would come and resurrect me. I want to say aloud, *I feel dead inside and need some miracle to give me hope again.*

My grandad, unlike me, had unbounded faith. He always talked about possibilities rather than obstacles. I was about twelve when I told him that the headteacher had asked me to talk about our new prime minister in front of the whole of year eight at the school assembly. I had asked him if I could be the head of the country and had added that, if so, I would remove all bad people from the world. He had replied, 'Always possible,' and squeezed my hand.

At the break, Joan finds me and introduces herself by her title, 'Chair of the BDG.' She has the same direct yet kind stare from our last encounter. She must know who I am, even with my five-day-old stubble, my printed white T-shirt and uncut curly hair. As she takes one step closer to me, someone interrupts her. She turns to introduce herself to another newcomer. I move back to my seat. My rise and fall with DigiArt floods back. As soon as the talk finishes, I mumble some excuse about having to get home to the person next to me. I am the first person out of the door. My mind is blurred. The talk sparked a little light in me. Seeing the paintings, albeit on a screen, was a pleasure for my eyes. But seeing Joan has triggered my pain of being forced out of the fourth floor.

I like to hide any down moments in my life. Weakness was never shown in the family. This was instilled by Mum as much as Grandad. When Dad died, Mum accepted it and within a month was her normal self. She had rolled her sleeves up and taken on a full role at the council. She said to my uncle once, 'Our culture shapes us to have many friendship circles, like a mandala, holding us together during difficult times.'

Anyway, there was no point relaying my troubles to my sister ... I am not sure if I trust her advice. Sure, Larissa was there for me during times of family strife. She once spent two nights by my bedside in the hospital when I had to have my appendix removed. But when it came to work, we compete like mad, neither of us wanting to be of lower status.

She would take my situation as a sign of weakness and have an upper hand. I wish Raff was here. I'd get guaranteed support. There is no-one to replace him.

That night, I have a dream of being trapped in the Uffizi gallery. I can't get out; every external door is locked. But I have the whole gallery to myself, forever.

The next day, I fill in my membership application to the BDG group. They meet fortnightly. I hope Joan will be too busy with her highly paid job to come to every meeting. The application form is a paper form that has been scanned into a digital version. The words *cheque payable to* are crossed out and the words *bank transfer* are written over them. I want to write a note to say a community app would be quicker and more marketable, but Joan might read it.

Cheque books disappeared five years ago. My grandad used to give me a cheque for my birthday when I was very young, with the cheque in my dad's name. I never knew what happened to the money. At thirteen, I felt blessed for he started giving me cash.

A few days later, I find the best parking spot, right near the entrance to the office lift. My car clock says 8:05 a.m. We have an early morning meeting to test our server contingency plans. The cleaner is wiping down the furniture. The meeting room light is on. I can hear people in conversation. The cleaner comes over to my desk.

'Have you moved from the fourth floor then? I asked about you and Tina said you had gone down. And that you don't work for that team anymore.' She is staring at my navy T-shirt.

My hands are still warming from the cool morning. My brain jitters from slumber.

She says, 'It's noisy here isn't it, do you like it?' She looks down at my dirty trainers. I last wore these when I took Nabin to football.

Bad thoughts flash in my head about my old team. I had not heard from Tina after I left, apart from her notification of removing my access rights to the slicing software. The cleaner puts her hand on her mouth. She mumbles something, turns her back and scutters away. That's the last time I ever speak to her. I look at the mirror after I relieve myself in the bathroom. My eyes are pink. I can see grey hair above my ears. And worst of all, I have a dislike of the person I see.

When I get home Nabin finds me. 'Dad, we need to put up some blinds. It's so bright early in the mornings.' Guilt overcomes me. I can't hide in my room today. He has a tape measure in his hand. We read the supplier's instructions, scrolling through each section on the iPad.

I say to Nabin, 'I remember Grandad told me that it's better to have some tolerance when measuring things rather than be exact.' He was repairing a chair and asked me to measure the length of the replacement wood, but he had adjusted the number by one centimetre. Only later had I understood what this meant.

Nabin nods, yet his eyes are blank. After some research, we agree the gap between the blind and wall should be between two millimetres and five millimetres. I place the order online with instructions about the blind width tolerance. Nabin goes back to his Airfix model, and I lie down on my bed.

After dinner, I clear and wipe the table as fast as possible as Mona boxes up tomorrow's lunch. I splay open the pizza pamphlet, dropped today from the letterbox. It picks up water from the damp table. On the front is a flash sign with the words *50% off all sizes*. I watch Mona replenishing the spice box. I want to hurry her up, so that I can speak.

When the last spice bowl is refilled in the box, I say, 'Shall we go to Egypt after the wedding? It's on our bucket list. I can get 10% off if we book by the end of the month.'

She closes the cabinet door and it thuds shut. The back of her ears are going red. The wave-like noise of the last rinse cycle from the washing machine is louder than normal.

She keeps her back to me. 'We have already been to Dubai. Another 5-star holiday that we can't afford isn't going to cover up the cracks, Aman.'

I fold up the damp pizza pamphlet. 'The time off would be good. Egypt is very hot nowadays. How about South America? It's on your list. Mexico, Cancun or maybe even Rio. The earlier I book, the better the deal.'

She turns around but remains at the sink. Her eyes are piercing into my forehead.

'You have lost your job and are on 70% of your old salary. We have a massive debt on your Amex Card. We haven't paid off the last holiday yet.'

I unfold the pizza leaflet as if I am talking to it. I say, 'I just thought we should have a break.'

She drags the chair out from the table. She takes the leaflet from my hand and places it at the far end. Her eyes close briefly.

'I know you have been suffering from the loss of Raff. But you have lost more than that. You refuse to accept reality or even face up to your feelings. Your head is not right!'

I don't like her being so blunt. I say, 'But you loved the Dubai trip. You said it was the best holiday since our honeymoon. I thought that's what it was all about!?' I shout out, 'Amazing experiences.'

My teeth are clenched. I want to thump the table. She puts her hand on top of mine.

It's warm and soft.

'Aman, I do enjoy the holidays, but I prefer to spend time together as a family day to day.'

I want to say, *But I am already taking Nadia to karate.*

She strokes my hand and says, 'Why don't we start doing things together again? Like playing squash? Remember, we did that for so many years after we got married. I am home earlier on Thursdays, and we both need the exercise.'

I squeeze her hand before releasing it and grab the pizza leaflet again. Mona is right, but at this moment I want to be on a beach being pampered by some attendant and looking at beautiful views to take the pain away in my stomach.

***

On Thursday, Mona and I drop Nadia at karate and head to the sports complex. We stop after three games. I am exhausted after only thirty minutes. Mona wins by 2–1, the scores 11–3, 10–12, 9–11.

Normally, I won in close matches, but today I don't care. There is no café, and the foyer has tatty plastic chairs. We share a bottle of Lucozade from the vending machine.

'Remember we used to do this after we got married?'

Mona shakes her head. 'What, talk about who played the better game?' She laughs and passes the Lucozade bottle to me.

'No, sit in the lovely café facing the pool at the private club and chat about everything and nothing. Now all we do is talk about work problems, finances and repairs.'

After a sip, Mona says, 'Do you know that there is a guy at work who brings his pet mouse with him?! It used to petrify me, but now the mouse just sits on his table, and he has his tiny cage, which he enters when his owner goes for meetings.'

I involuntarily dribble some liquid from my mouth.

'Apparently, there is no law against bringing pets, as long as they don't disrupt anyone.' Mona hands me a tissue.

I swallow what's left in my mouth, and then share my battles with the vending machine. For the first time in ages, we are both giggling spontaneously.

Nadia's face glows as she sees us entering the karate hall. Even the instructor seems pleased to see Mona and I together. We end up talking to two mums and a dad. None of whom I have met. On the final stretch of road as I drive back home, Mona turns around in her seat and makes a gesture to Nadia.

On cue she says, 'Dad, Kaya is feeling frustrated about the wedding. I think you should call her up and be more active in your support. She told me she is fed up with just text messages. You said you have more time now that you are in a different job. You always say that family is important, and we all know you have amazing planning skills.'

The next day, just before 9:30 a.m., an email is forwarded by my boss – he has added the words *update from our customer* in front. It's from the CEO: *We are delighted to announce that Tina Stephens has been promoted and will effectively be Shadow Director from the 1st of October. Her management of new product lines has been exemplary, particularly in balancing risk and opportunities. We all wish Tina every success.*

My teeth are grinding together, and my legs are shaking. I read the email again; there is no mention of my name. I created the foundation for this product, found new clients and built the key elements of infrastructure. The only person who values my skills now is Kaya.

I depart and head to Zeno's. I pick the biggest iced bun with my coffee and call Kaya using my ear set. She is a physiotherapist, but on Fridays, her morning is free. She teaches at a local college in the afternoon.

'Uncle, I have found the decorations, sorted out my dress. I am struggling with the invitation list, so worried I might miss someone. I can't make my mind up about the venue but have two booked tentatively. Worse than that, I have no idea about what food we should serve.'

She spends another five minutes talking me through all her doubts.

I interrupt – 'Part of the confusion is that you are not clear about the purpose of the wedding. What should the experience be for the guests? How do you want the different relatives and friends to share in your happiness on your day? This is more important than the venue and décor.'

There is a pause, and I imagine the whirr sound of the office server rooms going on in Kaya's mind.

'You are completely right,' she says, 'I haven't thought enough about the purpose.'

I reply, 'Let's talk next week, Wednesday at seven o'clock? If that works for you, I will gather a few people together.' I know what she will say next. So, I add, 'And that includes your Uncle Lekh.'

I have left my pen in the office. I grab the nearest serviette and borrow a pen from the plump lady at the counter. I write:

- *What is the wedding about for Kaya and Remi?*
- *How should the wedding be remembered?*
- *What will guests expect?*
- *What should we include/not include?*
- *Who will help with what?*

At my desk, I can't sit still. There is a swirling emptiness in my stomach, and I head to the vending machine. The D7 slot is empty, but I half expected it. I thump the machine with my palm. Who else is gobbling up sea salt crisps? I search for the next tastiest thing and press E4 where the mint creams are.

'Hey!'

I turn around. My shoulder is wonky. Emily's eyes are dancing.

'I was just coming to see you. Do you fancy a coffee? We haven't spoken for ages.'

A part of me wants to take her to Zeno's, but we head to the coffee shop. Annetta isn't there. Of course, Friday is the day of the week I've never seen her. Peter and the CEO are standing by the counter. They both wave to me as I join the queue. I search for bitterness in their faces but can't spot any. They have takeaway cups and depart as I order two lattes.

Three sips later, I wish I had just got some water. My head is throbbing. I stir my coffee. In the past, Emily and I would talk about work projects or her son. My ego wants her opening words to say Tina's management is not as brilliant as mine, like it's an undeniable truth. That would make me feel a foot taller. She looks at me like she wants me to do all the talking. The same way my mum does when I am in a bad mood. I keep stirring.

I say, 'I am fine on the second floor, it's all fine, I enjoy the peace and quiet.'

She looks under the table. I stop tapping my feet in a beat with the jazz music.

'How is your niece's wedding coming on? They must be loving your planning experience.'

I pull out the serviette from my pocket and translate my scribbles. Her eyes sparkle with understanding.

'Sunita? Is that your friend Raff's wife?'

I hadn't noticed I had scribbled her name on the serviette. 'Sunita has a soft spot for Kaya and used to babysit her from time to time when she was three years old. I was going to ask her to help. It will feel like having Raff with me.'

She nods like she understands perfectly.

How did your son's GCSE go?' I ask.

She looks at me; her face is calm. 'I took your advice about asking him to make a personal structure for study rather than seeing it as a number of hours. Well, he had a good plan and kicked a ball between study sessions. He said it helped him memorise things better. In the end, I was just around for support – I didn't bother him much.'

She looks down and laughs. 'The benefit for me is that my energy levels are much higher.'

I can't recall giving this advice. But it's easy for me to slip into offering ideas. I wonder if Nadia has her own method for studying.

On my way home, I find myself driving to Raff's house. I call Sunita a few minutes before I arrive. Nothing has changed on the road. The solar panels are shining from his neighbour's house as the last bits of sunlight hit them.

Sunita must have seen my car. She opens the door before I can touch the blue knocker. She stares at the stubble on my chin and then waves to the neighbour passing. There are even more photos of Raff and Simi in her house than when I last visited at the time of the funeral.

'The neighbours have been so good to me, you know, as has Raff's family. I hardly ever feel lonely. I miss Raff every day, yet he would be happy with how I've adjusted.'

She moves towards the corner full of pictures of Simi and comes back with one of Simi and Kaya, both toddlers. We spend the rest of the time talking only about the wedding.

That evening, I decide to have a shave. The last time was two weeks ago. I reduce my inch-long sideburns with a trimmer. There is more grey hair than black in the pedal bin. Afterwards I look at Botticelli's *Mars and Venus* more closely, noticing the symmetry of the forest behind Venus' head. The green in the trees is lighter than before.

That evening, Raff does not occupy my dreams.

CHAPTER 7

WEDDING PREPARATIONS

Wednesday comes around fast. That whole afternoon, all I do is make notes about the wedding plan on my app. I don't check emails for two hours, my all-time record. There is a recurring thought that Lekh will take over our gathering tonight.

When evening comes, everyone is there by 8:30 p.m., apart from Remi. According to Kaya, he is busy with some work deadline. He works in the glossy, money-driven world of corporate finance. I doubt he would ever understand the complexity and contradictions of Asian family weddings.

Mona insisted Mum should come. She said it would matter to have her there.

I sit in the middle of the largest sofa. Kaya sits on the right of Lekh who is opposite me. I wish she was sitting next to me. Sunita and Lekh are chatting like they last met yesterday. Nabin's on the sofa armrest and Nadia on the piano stool. The piano to my far right has not been touched since Nadia protested about grade exams a year ago.

I point to my Titian replica painting above the piano. It shows men and women across the ages, all as part of a musical scene.

I say in the general direction of Lekh, 'This picture is called *The Music Lesson*. From my understanding, it shows the passing of time amongst friends and family and the importance of being together.'

Lekh stands up to take a closer look.

I add, 'And Titian is keen to show this by presenting the musicians as amateurs.'

My cousin is examining the painting like he's checking on my description.

He returns, his eyes smiling. He nods and whispers, 'Nice.'

Kaya's fiancé, Remi, is the last to arrive. His tie is still on, his shirt is without a crease, and he is wearing his shoes as he enters the room. Grandad insisted that we leave our shoes at the door – a tradition that has stayed, at least in this house. I want to shake my head at Kaya – she could have told Remi. Mona is looking at Remi's feet like she is undressing his shining brogues. His grace period with her will be short.

The drinks are all laid out by Nabin on the central low oval coffee table. Larissa and my brother-in-law are on the video screen from Mauritius. On my 45-inch TV screen, Larissa's face is glowing with her tan. I hear the swish, swish sounds of the waves behind her beach apartment, and the movements of the thin white curtain behind her.

The serviette from Zeno's, with the five questions, is on my lap with my doodles on it.

'Let's work on the aim first. What's the wedding about for Kaya and Remi? What impression and experience do we want to give? More importantly, what will fit in with our family tradition?'

Kaya puts her hand briefly on Remi's thigh. 'Me and Remi have thought a lot on this. We realise the wedding is about the people in our lives and giving them an experience to remember. More than just a special day for us.'

I want to correct her English.

Her hand is flicking through her smartphone with pace.

She looks at Remi and continues, 'We have spoken to both sets of parents and we all feel tradition is important. We will have the full Buddhist ceremony. And we want it to be both sombre yet engaging.'

Larissa and my brother-in-law both nod from the screen like they have been primed by Kaya.

Lekh knows more about our family tradition than anyone in the room. My mum goes to the *Bāhā*, but mainly to socialise. Lekh, I suspect, goes every week for the sermon.

As Kaya opens her mouth, Lekh lurches forward, 'From our family's point of view, we need to keep the older generation happy. I remember the traditional blessings we had when you were born, Kaya, and of course at Larissa's, Aman's and my wedding.'

Kaya turns her feet towards Lekh. 'I want to do something that embraces my roots but also my Britishness. I don't want to divide up the two cultures and prefer to do something all in one.'

I jot *Buddhist/British* and the word *Scope* on my notes. My grandad's first joy of Britain was the Beatles, and after that, most pop. One of the most vivid memories from my wedding is him wearing the chequered Nepalese *ṭopī* and dancing to Spandau Ballet. His dance style was improvised and funny to watch.

I gaze around the room. 'Let me show you the work we have done so far: budgets, halls, entertainment, décor types.'

Kaya turns her shoulder at Lekh. I don't like the two of them sitting together.

Lekh says, 'Are we assuming the wedding must be inside? Why can't it be outside?'

There is silence. I can hear the swish, swish of the waves from the screen even louder, as if the tide has come right in.

My grandad was born in a border town in Nepal, but his father was born in India. I remember my grandad explaining to my dad when I was twelve that Buddhism did not treat marriage as a spiritual necessity like the Hindus. The role of the *bajrachāryas* and more elaborate ceremonies were to compete against the Hindu culture. After all, Nepal and India were neighbours. But weddings took place between October and April in our family. Always.

Nabin says, 'Why can't we, Uncle Lekh? It will be more fun in the summer!'

Nabin's neck is longer, and he looks taller than last month, even while sitting down. He looks at Lekh as if he was in charge.

Lekh says, 'The *bajrachāryas* at our *Bāhā* are flexible when it comes to weddings. I think we can convince them to bless our ritual outside, with the relevant artefacts. And anyway, from what I know of scripture, good dates for a wedding have nothing to do with the faith ... some of our traditions and conventions are probably a spillover from the Hindus.'

My sister goes on mute. Her arms wave in the way Grandad's did, as she talks to my brother-in-law. Then, her full face reappears on the screen and she does a thumbs up.

Lekh makes a call to his dad to get approval. He speaks in fluent Nepalbhasa. My mother nods as she listens in.

Within fifteen minutes, we move the wedding to the end of May.

'Always test assumptions,' I remember telling Louis in the office in February when we were looking at our Cloud providers. Our assumption that all our data assets were best on the Cloud turned out to be wrong. An expert had shown us that a hybrid approach – our more confidential content stored on our local servers – was the best solution.

I had mixed feelings about seeing Lekh again, but now I am glad he is here. He has a typical Nepalese name, which is true to its culture more than mine. My uncle, being the older of the two brothers, took it upon himself to preserve the tradition more. This has rubbed off on Lekh. One meaning of his name is 'to write.' It fits him well with his job at the council.

The last time I visited his house, a Union Jack coaster and a picture of the Queen at her Windsor family home were on his sideboard. My grandad worked in Aldershot when they immigrated. My uncle was an army chef for thirty-two years. Since his retirement, he lives with Lekh in the town next to Aldershot.

My name has no Nepalese roots. About fifteen years ago, I had found out from an online search that it was a common name in many Indian traditions. On confronting my mum, she told me it meant 'secure' in Sanskrit – a name she chose herself. Right now, I am the most insecure person in this room. No career after fifteen years of hard graft, virtually no friends, a large mortgage and only this wedding for my self-worth.

Nabin goes to the kitchen and returns with the *sel rōṭī*, a sweet, deep-fried bread made with rice flour. He had cooked it with the help of my mum in a *karaī,* just an hour ago.

Lekh looks at my mum and says, 'Auntie, you always made us these when I came around to your house, during holidays.'

I want to tell my mum that she hasn't made *sel rōṭī* for me for many months. Instead, I take a large bite.

The ideas start flowing, partly from the excess sugar in the *sel rōṭī*. Mona's idea is about having a choir to sing alongside the ritual. Sunita's is for everyone there to plant a tree, as a sign of progress and connection with nature. The one I share is having an artist to paint live scenes of activity. These would be digitised and sent to every family as a present. Nabin wants fun sports activities during the day. Altogether, we collate fourteen items on my iPad, and we agree to put them to a vote at the next meeting.

Our conversations subside a few minutes before 11 p.m. But no-one wants to leave.

Lekh gradually moves towards the front door. I shake his hand but want to give him a hug. When we were kids playing together,

I'd throw myself at him as soon as he opened the front door of his house. Lekh's mum would make some *sukkha rōṭī* on a traditional *tawā* and we would have them hot while we competed in football or badminton in his tiny garden. My dislike for Lekh is seeping away.

My mum, Sunita, Kaya, Nadia, Mona and my sister continue to chat about the formal wear for the occasion, while Nabin and I clear up. Remi's eyes are tinged red and struggling to stay open behind his rimmed glasses. A single *sel rōṭī* is in the *karaī*. My stomach is full, but I gobble it up involuntarily.

In the bedroom, I kick off my slippers and bounce on the bed with a sigh of pleasure. Mona looks at me as if I am drunk. She sips her hot lemon water. The bedside light switches off while I am still talking. I talk about the plans and personalities and how the wedding will flow. I hear her light snoring. That sets off my dread of going to work tomorrow. My hands have both rolled into a half fist.

The next day, I leave the office at 12:30 p.m. My plan is to go for a longer walk, as far away as possible, before getting a sandwich. From my left ear, I hear my name being called. It's the sound of someone I know, but not someone from work. I am fifteen steps past the coffee shop. I turn around. It's Annetta, the familiar face that normally greets me at the counter, but with her cap sticking out of her front pocket. She has a coffee stain on the palm of her hand.

'I am so sorry to bother you.' She gazes at her stained hand and moves it behind her back. 'I have almost finished my MicroMasters in Cloud Computing Architecture. You mentioned this was a thing to learn when we had that chat a few months ago?'

I can't recall saying anything like that to her. Still, my head is nodding.

'I have started applying for jobs and I have an interview coming up. I am so nervous.'

I take a step closer to her. 'Don't hide your great customer service experience from the coffee shop. You have practice in dealing with varied situations, all sorts of customers and demands.'

She nods three times, like one of the juniors at the office.

'Check out the organisation. See who does what there and prepare some examples of problem solving – that question is bound to turn up.'

It's the first time I have seen her outdoors. She has the same energetic look that I had twenty years ago. Not wearing a cap makes her skin look shinier.

I wave and turn around.

'Wait a minute,' she says, as she heads back to the shop and returns.

The shop door is left ajar. She returns with a piece of paper, on it a QR code.

Her eyes are smiling the way Nadia's did when she was five. 'There are enough here for four coffees. You can add these to your app.'

She pulls out the crimson cap from her pocket and hurries back inside.

***

A few days later, I get a text message from George. It's 10:30 a.m.

Fancy a brew at Zeno's? If so, see you in reception in ten minutes.

I have an urge to find out what's happening in the team. My thumb clicks a thumbs-up emoji, with the light brown colour.

At Zeno's I don't wait for him to add sugar to his tea, I ask how things are going with our new products.

He stirs, not looking at me. 'All is well, had two interesting deals on the table, one with Taiwan and a small distributor in India, but otherwise it's the same old, same old.'

I know that already from Emily. The sugar will have blended in by now. Yet he still stirs.

He puts the spoon on the table. 'I miss our chats and banter, mate, I haven't seen you for over a month. You settled in on the second floor?'

I don't know whether to say the truth or pretend that I enjoy technical work.

A person in a suit, but no tie, comes right up to George. The buttonholes in his suit are rounded, which tells me it's an expensive hand-sewn type. His shoes are brown brogues, with the second row of stitching reflecting its quality Goodyear welt. He slaps George on his back.

They talk about the football results and a plumbing job the man needs advice on.

George gestures towards him as the man departs. 'He works for a finance company two buildings away from ours. I met the guy about a month ago and we started chatting. He's always sharing something or other.'

I regard my knowledge of people skills as quite good, but George excels in them.

'How do you do it, George? What's the secret to getting on well with everyone?'

He stares at his cup and then looks up. He replies, 'I bet you have just one or two friends you can count on?'

I swirl the coffee in my cup. I lift my head up. 'That's probably true.'

'Because mate, you see friendship as a scale, with some close and some further away.' He moves his arms apart. 'Like different objects on a ruler,' he says.

I half nod without thinking.

'Mate, friendships are like an onion,' he says, his hand shaped into a ball. 'They are kinda layered, give support to each other and all make the onion a whole.'

I have saliva in my throat. I envy George.

He continues, 'Let me give you an example. All the dads at my daughter's football club meet once a month at the pub. What's interesting is we're all supporters of different clubs – from Chelsea, Man U and even Arsenal – and the banter is loads of fun. Sometimes we share a personal experience or difficulty. Someone usually chips in with good advice or sometimes just a nod.'

He takes another sip from his tea, pushes away the almost-full cup. He says, 'Tastes like weak piss today. I bet you they are trying some snobby new tea.'

He goes up to the counter, waves his hands in a quick motion, but speaks softly. He comes back with another cup of tea. It has steam rising from its top. He smells it.

'Effing nice now. The other thing, mate, I have learnt, is to be on good terms with neighbours. My neighbour two doors down at no. 25 convinced me to try out volunteering with an animal sanctuary he works for. I love it. We go once every fortnight for a few hours. It's a nice mix of fun. In fact, I met the guy who fixed my leaking roof there.'

I don't like being called *mate* so many times.

At the till, he orders eight large, iced buns to share with my old team. I have a sugar rush as it's being packed at the counter. The icing on it is generous and snow white. I am beginning to understand the mind of George and his behaviour. He looks down and then up.

'Shall we do a brew every two weeks, mate? I'd love to tap into your mind on some of that strategy mapping you go on about.'

He looks at his shoes. His voice is a bit shaky. 'And also, I want some career advice on where I go next.'

At the entrance barrier, I wave my pass, ignoring the receptionist. George goes up to her to have a chat. I stop at the lift and turn back. George looks at me, his eyebrows raised.

I mumble, 'See you later, mate, I need to pop back out for something.' I can't believe I used the word *mate*.

I return to Zeno's. The lady serving raises her eyebrows, like I left something. My debit card is already out. I order ten iced buns.

As soon as I get to the second floor, I write on a pink Post-it Note, *Help yourself… from Zeno's.* The buns are on a small round meeting table. The guy who sits three desks to my right is the first one up. He works for the support team. It's been six weeks since I've sat here. Until today, he never had a social chat with me. He bites into the icing, looks at me and tells me about the doughnut shop his kids like.

On my way to the next BDG meeting on Monday, the Central line has a fifteen-minute delay. 'Man under train' is what the guard tells me on the platform. I ask, 'Suicide attempt?'

He raises his eyebrows like it's a common occurrence. 'Who knows? Could be. People do stupid things.'

I see an image of a man, an office worker in brown brogues, and a shirt with no creases, squashed under a rail. Maybe from all his commitments with no hope. Or perhaps he lost all the respect of his family, and they threw him out and he wanted a fast track to a new life.

When I get to the basement, the image of an office worker is still rolling inside my head. Joan is already there, her back straight and sitting in the front row, on the far right. I sit on the back left.

The talk is on Botticelli's *Primavera*. The speaker says, 'Many people miss one aspect of Botticelli's painting, in Florence. That is that there are over four hundred plants and flowers in the dark layers of canvas. According to some, there are two hundred and fifty species of flowers alone. They may be in the background, but they make a visual whole.'

She continues, 'Scholars disagree, but some say this painting is a sign of neo-platonic love. Thus, intense attachment symbolised by

Zephyrus, this winged god on the right, is renounced by Venus. She turns her back on Zephyrus and Cupid at the top and then gazes at Mercury on our left.'

I like this description. It reminds me of the conversation with George. Is Botticelli trying to say all types of relationships are important, not just those formed through wedlock?

At the break, I find myself edging towards Joan who is chatting to two men. I sip a flavoured drink from a thin plastic cup.

She addresses three of us. 'I had an instant attraction from my visit to the Uffizi fifteen years ago. It was the best thing I did on the rest day of my international fencing tour.'

I nod. Botticelli's painting grabbed me in the same way, when I had first seen it in my twenties.

I say, 'Don't you think there must be some deep well within the painter, for him to visualise and recreate so much?'

Joan says, 'Well, it's also the environment. At the time, the Medici's money attracted immense creative talent, fresh thinking and spontaneity. His wealth, their platonic idealism, brought a myriad of artists that collaborated on their paintings and art. It must have been the catalyst for Botticelli's genius to shine through.'

Joan turns to speak to someone else. I have a daydream. *Primavera* is on display on the second floor, on the wall opposite my desk. I am admiring it. I try to explain its meaning and depth to my colleagues and we have a conversation about the use of lapis lazuli, the rare aquamarine blue.

'Time to go start again, folks.'

I am standing alone. The plastic cup is still full in my hand. Everyone else is already sitting for part two.

Joan calls out for me when I leave the building. She is buttoning her cream jacket on the pavement. We are in stride for five minutes, heading towards the same station. She must know from her underlings, who administer the contract with DigiArt, that I have been sacked. I talk and keep the chat on the art and my possible maiden visit to the Uffizi in Florence. We stop at the bottom of the stairs. We are on different tube lines. I make a fist from happiness. The conversation won't meander towards my job. I sigh as soon as she is out of sight. I like Joan – but every time I see her, I am triggered about my past glory.

***

In mid-October, we reconvene for the wedding planning meeting. I can hear the 'dhunk' sound of water running in the central heating pipes. It's the first time since March we've had the central heating on.

Lekh arrives first. He has a Buddha bust with the ultramarine blue hair. It looks familiar. He heads straight over to my mum who is standing by the living room door. He bows.

'Auntie, you gave this to me, as you knew I liked it so much. But it's time to return this to you. I think we should have it as part of the wedding décor, maybe on the side table next to the ceremony. I will miss it. I look at it every day, you know, as it's right on the windowsill by my front door.' He glances at me. 'It always makes me calmer.'

I glare at my mum. 'I did wonder where Buddha went.'

I take the statue from my mum and touch the blue hair. It is the same colour as the sky of the Titian painting I saw at the National Gallery. I place the statue on top of the piano and take my place on the sofa.

Kaya nudges Lekh. He says, 'It is important to have everything flow at the wedding. We need to keep things moving for every ritual and activity to keep guests informed and engaged while still ensuring they enjoy the moment.'

Remi is in his navy socks. His brogues will be by the door. He is still in his work suit, but without a tie.

Kaya nods, then Remi, and everyone else nods in unison.

Lekh is saying what I would have said, but in a simpler way. I don't like not being in charge, but I do feel less burden on my shoulders.

We all discuss which person will take on which activities. These include venue, décor, liaising with the *Bāhā*, catering, entertainment, invitations and ushering.

I talk about the RACI method, something I use on all projects. It is a grid showing all the key activities as rows on the left and the names of all the people as column headings. I already have a template that I used when I was managing new products on the fourth floor. I fire it up on my iPad. I see the names of my full team: Emily, Louis, George, all the IT guys and Peter. I feel my heart beating and warm. I want to be back with the team on the fourth floor, in that space and rhythm. I save the spreadsheet as *Kaya – Wedding* and change the names. I wish Emily was here with us.

During the break, everyone is served a bowl of mango ice-cream with wafers. Mona got them from the oriental supermarket yesterday. It's made with *maldahā* mangoes, loved by Grandad for their sweetness. I am in a huddle with Remi and Lekh, plus my virtual sister on the wall. Everyone else is chatting in the kitchen. Larissa opens her eyes wider as she sees Lekh next to me.

'How are things going in your new director role, Aman?' Her voice sounds like she is in a work meeting.

'Fine,' I reply, glad Mona or my mum haven't mentioned my situation yet.

Her eyes are moving right and back again. 'Well, I wanted to let everyone know, I got promoted to Senior Director over here. It now means a 120-strong team and more travel in the Southern Hemisphere, mainly South Africa, Botswana, Kenya and, of course, Australia.'

I give a silent clap. Lekh's body is still. Larissa's face is beaming. Her ears are pointing up. At our last family call, I had mentioned my promotion and my vision. She was playing the same competitive game as me. I want to jump into the sea behind her.

My dad liked it when Larissa and I competed, whether at board games or some random argument. He only intervened when things got out of hand.

Lekh's eyes are staring into my walnut wooden floor. I know he finds the corporate world shallow and greedy. It's one of the things Larissa and I argued with him about during our teenage years, which carried on until our early twenties. He had no interest in joining a brand. He told Larissa and me many times that we were obsessed with money and status. I tried to put him off from working for the council. He still works there, handling planning permissions. Lekh has never been on a foreign holiday, apart from visiting Nepal every year. He has not an inch of ambition and yet finds happiness in doing his repetitive work. I have a lump in my throat. Lekh has a high status in the borough and all the security in the world. I am the one at a dead end.

The arguments our dads had were always about money and its value. My dad had this story that I know by heart:

'When I was a little boy in Nepal, nobody looked at me. They looked at my shoes, which were handed down by your uncle. Both had a hole by the little toe. It didn't matter how much I polished and patched up the holes, everyone spotted the defect. I was ashamed. That's why money is important. It buys you respect.' He would pause to look at his dark brown polished brogues. Dad had paid £150 for them – a fact etched in memory. He would continue, 'My brother sees poverty as the law of karma. I believe in the Buddha, but only effort got me these brogues.'

When I turned thirteen, Dad bought me the finest pair of shoes from Clarks. My geography teacher noticed, and a couple of girls smiled at me.

When we reconvene, Kaya says, 'Let's discuss the actual ceremony. I am confused about what is essential and what isn't.' At my wedding, I had asked the same question and remember the varied answers. There is silence.

Sunita must sense the tension. She laughs and says, 'I hear that your ceremonies are elaborate and full of pomp. And that they take a long time.'

Lekh says, 'It's not necessarily long for Buddhists. The Hindu culture is sometimes intertwined with ours, but we don't need the elaborateness of a Hindu wedding. We don't have to have blessings from gods. More and more rituals have crept in from the Indian traditions.'

Lekh always knows the history of our customs better than me. I don't like that he has the upper hand.

'And the seeping in of Hindu rituals has happened over centuries like it has for other *śramaṇic* religions.'

I want to ask Lekh what *śramaṇic* means. Mona puts her hand on my thigh. I keep schtum.

Lekh says, '*Bajrachāryas* will be needed to conduct the ceremony. That won't be an issue – they seem to be plentiful around London; so many people of Newar in the big city.'

Larissa's nod can't be missed on the screen.

Lekh says, 'As per Kaya's request, he must speak excellent English as well as Nepalbhasa. And translate every word for the people present.'

I have been to around twenty Buddhist weddings in my lifetime, for family or friends of the family. Once, I met a cousin for the first time on their wedding day. This tradition of keeping in touch through the generations is not something I continued. My LinkedIn profile has 725 connections; many have taken me time to nurture. Yet, I know only a few family names and only those close to my grandad. Lekh is in touch with more family members than I am. I know that because he talked to more people than me at the last wedding. It's worse than that. Mona has built up healthy relationships from the moment I introduced her to my family. Sometimes, she has to remind me of who my cousins are.

Mona says, 'An outdoor wedding means we have more flexibility on the numbers we can invite, and this can be a positive thing.'

We go around the room for menu suggestions. The range covers every section of the globe. Lekh waits for everyone to finish. 'Do you remember the *chānā chatpat* your mum used to make every time I came around?'

'She made it especially for you, as she knew you loved it,' says my sister.

Lekh laughs. 'Well my mum made varieties of *tarkārī* when your family came around, do you remember? There was never anything left in the pot. Then she learnt to hide some of it, so that there would be some left when she joined us.'

'*Chānā chatpat* would be a hit as a starter, don't you think? And so easy to make.'

No-one protests, and Lekh asks me to add it to the list. The taste of chickpeas, cumin, cucumber with masala, all mixed, is a constant from my childhood. I want Mum to make it for me tomorrow.

Remi doesn't look unhappy with our choices; it probably ticks his box for an authentic wedding. He seems to take a liking to what Lekh says. But I don't want to end up with just traditional food. That would be so boring, just a repetition of other weddings.

'Let's get more ideas for the menu – we don't have to agree on everything today.'

Kaya gives me a fist bump, like we used to during the pandemic. A teardrop is forming in her right eye. She goes round the room and gives everyone a hug. I remember this feeling; it matches the time we took her to Chessington theme park when she was seven years old. She had gone round the small rollercoaster four times and knew the jingle that went with it by heart. And she cried from joy on the journey home. That lost feeling of elation returns in my heart. I hope it never leaves. Remi shakes my hand like he has just had a spoon of sugar.

I take the Buddha bust and put it on the front door window-sill. All religions are full of contradictions, Raff had said to me. But right now, I like contradictions. Lekh and I are so different. I stare at the Buddha's supine nose. My dad stopped going to the temple the minute he turned eighteen. But he always had this Buddha statue in his home office. Dad lost a lot of his money in the share market crash in the 90s. But this never made him return to the *Bāhā*. Instead, he worked harder. Within three years, he had pride back on his face.

My mum always complained of Dad's overwork.

That evening, I dream of being back at the *Bāhā* with Lekh by my side. We are both in a sermon facing a statue of the Buddha with blue hair.

The next morning, the pleasure of the last evening is erased. Like the joy of a good movie that ends once the credits roll.

CHAPTER 8

CONNECTION

———————

A few weeks ago, the clocks went back, but the temperature is still at 19°C. When I was growing up, this was the time when all my jackets came out. So far this week I have walked every day to the park to eat my sandwich. I search every day for the old lady, but it's not until Thursday that I spot her sitting on a bench at the edge of the park. I clear my throat. There is a scarf on her shoulder. Her light cream jacket is buttoned. She puts down her *Metro* newspaper. She has a silver Parker ballpoint pen in her left hand. Her crossword has scribbles in the white space around it. It's three-quarters finished.

She gazes into my eyes and gestures twice, an order for me to sit down. Then right on cue she nods.

'I hate my job. It's so boring and repetitive; I can get it all done within three days of a week. I'm hoping they will want me back on the fourth floor, but I know it's a pipe dream. Worse than that, I have to force myself to start looking for new jobs. My CV looks awful with the demotion.'

She is staring at the granite track in front of us. She points to the snail trails – thin white stripy lines like someone has rubbed a glue stick on the path. One of the white lines extends as far as I can see.

She laughs. 'One snail has stamina.'

At last, she looks at me. 'I can't help you resolve your predicament.'

I hadn't heard the word *predicament* since I was at school.

She says, 'My only tip is whatever the situation, be attentive, even to the mundane.'

Before I can respond, she changes the topic. 'I can't receive any internet in the kitchen, and I've switched the box on and off, but it's not any better.'

I have no idea, but I find a YouTube video on what might be the issue and translate the three actions to her. She thanks me and looks back at the gravel. It goes quiet. I stand up. I remember I need to get a report to my boss. I say goodbye on the move. Her face is serene. She waves back like she understands. She takes out her newspaper, unfurling it in a way that people with time on their hands do.

At the zebra crossing, a self-driving car glides to a stop for me to cross the road. This is the third one I have seen this year. Despite my faith in technology, I keep my gaze on it, at every step. I had told Louis, during one of our chats, that there is still a risk of failure, even after endless testing. Unknown circumstances can develop anytime.

It's taken twelve minutes to get back to my desk. My breathing is uneven. There is an old-style Post-it Note stuck to my screen: *You forgot to send the monitoring analysis for the B6 server load; please send them immediately on your return. PS. This has happened a few times.* It's signed by the Head of Technology.

The deadline was plain in my calendar. My mind is filled with BDG meetings, planning the wedding, my career and wondering how things are on the fourth floor. Yet, how could I have missed this obvious task? I want to thump myself. My legs feel weak. I wish I could lie down on the wooden floor.

That night, I toss and turn. I see myself writing an apology to the Head of Technology. But what I want to do is send a resignation letter with concise bullet points of reasons.

***

I hear Mona's BMW drive past our window. I force my eyes open. The clock says 8:04 a.m. I jump up and open the curtains. I can see the postman across the road in his shorts and red jacket. He must be about five years older than me and probably on half my salary. He is talking to the neighbour at no. 47. The one with the loft conversion. They both laugh. Whenever he hands me a parcel at the door, he has something witty to say. I hope he doesn't knock today.

Half an hour later, I open my front door, and the neighbour's son is standing by my car in his school uniform. He is knocking his shoes on my wheel rim. I move towards him, and he stops, walking backwards towards his front door. His eyes are wide open, and his pupils are dancing.

I check the tyres, they look fine, but I feel deflated. As the car reads my fingerprint, I turn around. The kid is watching me. I want to say something but can't find any words. There is enough trouble in my life already. As the 'wrrrrr' of my electric motor comes to life, I start a podcast – *All Things Art*. There is a fresh episode every Wednesday.

As I take my foot off the handbrake pedal, the boy knocks on my window. The reinforced grey glass comes down slowly.

He pokes his head in. He says, 'I really like the shape of your car.'

His pupils are still moving in a circle. I give him a wave and wish him a nice day at school. Nabin also said that when I bought this car. Maybe the kid wasn't bad after all. I remember Raff's words when I gave him a dump of all the things that were annoying me. He said, 'Listen, you can't make such fast judgements about people. You think they are being deliberately obnoxious, but sometimes you misunderstand them or their motives.' My reappraisal of George fitted with Raff's advice.

I recall an email yesterday sent by the Director of Technology requesting a meeting at 8:30 a.m. We sit in his office at 10 a.m. I blurt out an apology. He looks deliberately stern.

'I am not sure what's happened to your discipline. It's like you have lost interest. We are very lucky to have your expertise, Aman. The team here likes you. I want to straighten things up so we can move on ...'

I would love to move on. He shuffles and closes his laptop lid.

'But I must give you a formal warning. It's in our company procedures. And I must tell you, that if it happens again, then you will be ...' he looks up, 'suspended pending investigation.'

His words are like being punched in the stomach. My credit card balance is huge, and I won't be able to pay mortgage payments on Mona's salary alone. I want to shout *pāgal*. It's the only swear-like word we were allowed when growing up.

He breaks into a smile. 'Don't take it so bad, Aman. It's a formal thing I have to say.'

I put my hands over my face briefly. He holds his right hand up.

He says, 'You look petrified, Aman. Just put your head down and focus on the work. You and I both know it's not difficult for a man of your abilities.'

I haven't had a job interview since I started applying a few weeks ago. It may take ages to get another role. Worse still, I don't have any self-respect.

My first bite of an iced bun at 11:30 a.m. releases a tiny pleasure wave in my mind, but it doesn't last more than a few seconds.

Fear drives me to check that my work for the rest of the week is on schedule. I hardly used to say the *shit* word, but I keep repeating it in my head interchanged with *pāgal* again and again as I pound on my keyboard. My dad had drummed many things into me and my sister.

One of them I know by heart from his repetition: 'Your self-respect is the most important thing. Bad work is shameful.'

As I munch my third iced bun, an email at the bottom of the screen in my unread list gets my attention. It's from Louis, on the fourth floor: *Boss, hope all is well with you and your new job. I am a bit concerned about the risk setting of our Cloud provider for the fashion products. They say the chances of an internet outage is very low, according to them (< 0.1%). But I read in the FT that there have already been two internet outages this year. What's your view? P.S. I have a meeting with Tina in over an hour, so appreciate a response if you pick this up in time?*

My reply says: *Low level risks need management, just because they are very unlikely to happen doesn't mean they won't. I'd get a second opinion on the risk threat. My view is that you should create a contingency plan for an outage of two hours.*

At 2:04 p.m., he sends me another email: *Just came out of the meeting. You are spot on Boss. We have agreed to take on a few hours' consultancy time with an expert and review the supplier's network. Will approach your recommended expert. Tina liked this approach in contingency thinking. P.S. I didn't mention you, as I'm not sure whether to or not ... I hope you don't mind but I got all the kudos. Anyway, thanks.* ☺

I jump up and pat the side of my bum. I want to roll into a ball and cry with joy. The guy opposite raises his eyebrows. But his keyboard rhythm does not pause. The office walls had been closing in on me since 10 a.m. this morning. Now they move a little bit away.

The following week, I leave the office at 4:45 p.m. I had already run out of work to do by 2 p.m. I arrive half an hour early for the BDG meeting. Joan is by the basement door, entering a combination code on the keypad. We are the only two people there. I help her lay out the drink tables with 'made from concentrate' juice and flaky plastic glasses. Her eyes are focused like she is solving some mystery as she sets the table. She lifts her head and her eyes widen.

'I bumped into Peter last week at the contract renewal meeting. He mentioned you have moved on to more technical work with a supplier. It's a pity as I so liked the way we shaped that proposal a few months ago.'

Every syllable of what she said is clear, like she had planned it. I feel like putting my head in my hands but force myself not to. Before I can respond, she moves to the opposite side of the room and puts the plastic wrapping in the bin.

When she returns, she says, 'Do you know my surname is Preston and yours is Pradhan. Isn't it funny that the two letters of our surname coincide with Sandro Botticelli's *Primavera*?'

I breathe out hard, laugh aloud. I want to say, *Many people have surnames with P followed by R*, but I want to impress Joan. 'Things aren't always coincidences. My grandad told me that chance and fate are completely linked. Perhaps it was meant to be that we ended up liking *Primavera*.'

Joan's stunning high cheekbones appear as she shakes her head. She must use one of those expensive Kensington dentists. I wonder if dentists' first names disproportionately start with 'D' and make a mental note to ask my AI app on my way home.

The table with the plastic cups and orange juice is furthest away from the entrance. It's the best spot to observe people as they come. Ten minutes later, they start wandering in – a whole variety. Some in suits, others in tatty jeans. Some extrovert to the quiet note takers. I spot a thin man who always wears a tie. He is a regular. He doesn't speak to anyone and finds the first possible space in a vacant chair. Somehow, though, we are all united by our love for Botticelli. In my meetings so far, not one person has asked me about my profession.

Today's talk is about the colours of paint used at the time of Botticelli and his fellow artists. My mind starts wandering.

The speaker says, 'The colours used by Botticelli were the finest pigments of his time. That included Vermilion, ultramarine and, of course, Verdigris green which were also often glazed. I will also explain how, over time, some colours have naturally darkened on paintings.'

That was too many colours for my mind to process.

'Many of you will know about the restoration of *Primavera* in 1982. One important aspect of the restoration was the removal of a yellowed varnish that had been applied to the painting in the nineteenth century. This varnish had made it difficult to see the details of the figures.'

I reach for my phone to check for messages.

'What we see now is a likeness to the original. Most experts agree that the background forest and fauna are darker than the original. The original would have had more of a Verona green while, due to ageing, we now have a much darker green.'

I sit up and put my phone back in my pocket. This makes sense; something about the colour isn't right. I know the forest is meant to convey a sense of growth, renewal and rebirth. And that is associated with the arrival of spring, but the dark colour is a contradiction.

On Wednesdays, the Head of Technology is in all-day meetings. For the last two Wednesdays, I have eaten my sandwich lunch on the tube and visited the National Gallery, which is five stops away. No-one has noticed that I am away for ninety minutes.

At the top end of Trafalgar Square, the security guard gives me a wave of familiarity. As I feel the warmth of the blower at the entrance, I glance back. The guard is my age and, apart from his glasses and his larger girth, he looks like me. He is polite to every visitor with bags in the security queue. His job can only be boring, but he acts like he likes it. I want to ask him if he is from Nepal.

My standard route has come about by intuition. I stay in the left wing, with the Renaissance paintings, pick a couple at random and then depart from the Gothic section, scanning a painting or two. My thirty minutes at the gallery lift me longer than eating iced buns. Today, I choose Jan van Eyck and his *The Arnolfini Portrait* from 1434. It shows a well-dressed couple in their reception room.

The brown clog shoes on the wooden floor in the foreground remind me of Grandad's pair. He had them posted from Nepal at a great cost. He used to wear them outdoors in the summer. There was a 'clomp' sound that came from them, and we could tell where he was in the house just from its volume. I follow Joan's tip. I move my eyes from top left to bottom right, zigzagging across. Oranges on the table, which must have been rare at the time, the ornate bed and sofa in the reception room and the most beautiful chandelier. All show the trappings of money. But the floor has no end-to-end carpet and the wall behind them has plain plaster. So, it must signify an up-and-coming couple, rather than one born into wealth. Their features are stern, as if not much lies underneath the exterior showing of status. I shiver despite having my thick jacket on.

I sense warm breath close to me. A couple are behind me, their heads protruding towards the picture. I have one last look and step back. The crimson colour of the bedspread is one of the colours on the Nepalese flag. I wonder if we can find similar coloured seats for Kaya's wedding. I have a vivid image of a row of red chairs all laid out in a green space with trees.

***

It's a grey gloomy day in December. At this time of the year, I don't like the speed at which days get shorter every day. I stopped walking up the two floors last week, as I found myself always short of breath. Emily is waiting in the lobby for the lift with a large paper cup. Her face looks tired. It matches the grey morning outside.

I say, 'How are things on the fourth?'

She replies, 'A bit stressful. Tina is about to go on urgent leave for three weeks to spend time with her mum. She lives in the Caribbean.'

Emily continues, 'Her mum has some sort of kidney issue. Apparently, it's terminal. Tina was crying in the ladies' yesterday.'

For a minute, I feel a pain in my heart. I can imagine Tina's suffering and what she will have to endure once her mum goes. But quickly, my mind takes over. Is there a possibility of being asked to return to my old job? Maybe some arrangement can be made to quit my second-floor job. That day and the next, I check my email and texts every thirty minutes, hoping for a note from Peter.

Two days later and I have heard nothing. My head feels hot, and I suddenly realise I'm angry – angry at my own pure selfishness. I fire an email to Tina, adding two sad emojis.

A few days later, I get forwarded an email from Emily. It is from Peter: *Tina Ward has taken urgent leave for a personal matter. In her absence, Louis Garcia will be taking on the temporary leadership of New Products. I know the whole company will support Louis during Tina's absence.*

I head to the ground floor and sit in the toilet cubicle. My head is in my hands. Bits of bread from breakfast are regurgitating in my upper digestive tract.

My breath is loud and uneven. Louis has been picking my brains for many months now. I want to confront Peter but also congratulate Louis, as if I were his full-time mentor.

The rest of the day, the flow of traffic is louder. I glance several times at the large window. I want to jump out and join the noise of the traffic underneath. My pain would be gone in an instant. One of my team members is hovering over my desk.

He holds two iced buns in a brown bag. 'Look what I got you from Zeno's. It was my turn.'

Once the whole bun is in my stomach, I stop looking at the window.

On the drive home, I flip between stations for the latest news. The headlines are about two escaped Asian elephants from an Anglian safari park. The wardens are finding it hard to shepherd them back. I turn the volume up. I am glad my mind has something else to focus on. The reporter plays out the story in a farmer's field from the live location. I can pick out the distressed sounds of the elephants blaring from the powerful subwoofers of my car. I want the elephants to keep their escape plan going. It must be lovely to be able to roam without restriction. My cousin sent me a photo last year of a family of Nepalese elephants near his town having a mud bath.

I have visited Nepal three times. The last time when I was twenty-two. I had stayed at my cousin's house and gone with Mum and Larissa. My cousin had a family of five in his tiny two-bedroom flat with small double beds in each bedroom. We had rations of one bucket of hot water each for our wash. Mum and Larissa slept in one of the bedrooms. I slept on the floor on a coir mattress. My cousin slept next to me, like he wanted me not to be alone. It felt both weird and nice, like being in a dormitory. My back hurt every morning.

I could not cope with all the piled-up rubbish outside on the road. It irritated me and I kept asking my cousin whose job it was to collect it. Worse than that, three days after arriving, I had a week-long bout of diarrhoea that lessened the joy of the mountain views and the beautiful *Boudhanāth Stūpa* a half hour away from Kathmandu. All I can remember is the Buddha's wisdom eyes painted on the top of the tower. We had caught the plane home the day after I had recovered.

My cousin still asks us to visit every time we have an interaction. In his last message, he had written in Nepali, which I can understand a bit better than traditional Nepalbhasa. I still had to get a translation from my AI app: *Kathmandu is good now. Your brother Lekh loves coming here. Now we have moved into large flat. No rubbish on our streets. Now a whole bedroom with an attached bathroom for your family.*

Nabin is at home when I return at 5:50 p.m. Nadia has gone to my mum's. It will be at least an hour before Mona arrives.

Nabin sees the blank look on my face as I sit on the sofa and says, 'Dad, let's play a game we learnt during drama studies today. We use random words and create a story. The sole rule is to say "yes and" before the start of each turn. Give me two random words.'

I say, 'Cloud computing and elephant.'

He starts with, 'One day, there was an elephant in the forests of Nepal.'

'Yes, and he had nowhere to go for a wee and so decided to use a large well nearby.'

Nabin continues, 'Yes, and with the amount of liquid and the warm day, a huge cloud appeared above the elephant's head. Just above that cloud, a demigod appeared. It started doing some calculations.'

I continue, 'Yes, and now we call this kind of situation Cloud computing.'

We both laugh, our tummies moving in sync.

'This is fun, Nabin.'

He says, 'Well, in drama class, they say this game is good for freeing up the mind and seeing possibilities. Actors sometimes use this warm-up before going on stage to prepare for surprises.'

I say, 'And maybe seeking improvisation possibilities in preparing for plays.'

Nabin nods in agreement.

I like this game. I say, 'Okay, let's do a story connecting the words job, colour and Botticelli.'

Nabin gives a big thumbs up. I ask him to start.

'One day, a man called Botticelli, who lived in Florence, was going to be interviewed for an interesting job as a painter.'

I imagine the colours in the *Mars and Venus* painting on the landing. I reply, 'Yes, and at the interview, he didn't know what to say when asked about his view of Verdigris and Malachite.'

Nabin frowns. I mouth the word *colour.*

Then he lets out a short laugh. He says, 'Yes, and that was because Botticelli had no view on any colours; he simply painted in the moment.'

I reply, 'Yes, and because of this, he kept failing at interviews – so, in the end, he employed himself by painting pictures and selling them to a friend.'

Nabin finishes with, 'Yes, and that's how the word "start-up" was invented; it all started in the Renaissance.'

I high-five my son, and he starts to giggle. I follow his cue. The last time we had such a moment was when he was five. We were playing hide and seek with the rest of the family. We had hidden behind a suitcase inside my wardrobe. We tried not to giggle but could not stop. Mona had played along for ten minutes trying to find us. By the time she did, Nabin and I were both in tears, and the inside of the wardrobe was a mess.

Maybe working for a start-up is something I should consider. I have only ever worked with large organisations.

Grandad held a steady government job in Kathmandu, but on the weekends, he used to take out his bicycle rickshaw and hang around fancy restaurants to get customers. He had noticed that a lot of his fellow drivers' bikes sometimes lost a chain or had a puncture, resulting in upset customers. So, he quit driving a rickshaw and started repairing them instead. I remember his broken English: 'I fix my friend's bike, and the day after, I fly my first plane to London.'

After dinner, I open my laptop on the kitchen table. Mona is talking about her day. She talks about each of her operational problems. I nod to her every few seconds, but I am not paying any attention. I search for recruiters in senior management who focus on technology start-ups.

Mona stretches her neck to see what I am doing and sees the title of my current role – *Technology Manager (Secondment)*.

She says, 'You should be truthful about your current role. I thought you said that your grandad taught you never to lie.' She laughs as she reads my CV.

She says, 'Secondment, eh ... anyway, you will get found out at the interview.'

'Well, it's all true, I am sure they will ask me to rejoin DigiArt, once Tina messes things up.'

I know that this will never happen, things will never be like they used to be. I am lying in hope.

Mona, like she has heard my thoughts, pats me on the back.

'Good thing you are not working for my manager at the hospital. She can spot a fake from a mile away!'

***

One of my responsibilities for this wedding is to help finalise the venue. Kaya, Nadia and I visit Bushey Abbey on Sunday. The buildings of Bushey village are hidden by the circle of old oak trees in the circumference of the estate. We drive past the automated main gates. Even though it's winter, the estate's upkeep means the scent of freshly cut grass seeps through the car's ventilation. The lush foliage and the darker green trees remind me of the backdrop of *Primavera*.

During our walk, the manager says, 'The trees are of three varieties: oak, elm and pine. And we have many cornflowers that will be blooming next May.'

I remember the talk at a BDG meeting. Cornflower, a purple petal variety, was abundant in *Primavera*, both on a dress and being part of the foliage. So perhaps the painting was depicting the time of May rather than early spring from its title. I have an instant affinity for the venue.

Kaya says, 'When Remi and I last visited we fell in love with this place.'

The ground space is huge, and there are many places we could conduct the ceremony, outside or inside. What's more, there is a small but pristine lake one hundred metres from the abbey. We trek around the grounds, trying to find a spot for the wedding. There are no built-up areas to be seen from this vast estate. No-one would believe we are in a suburb.

Kaya makes a video call to Remi. She gets his approval ten minutes later. Kaya, Nadia and I stand in a triangle at the possible location of the wedding *maṇḍapa*.

Kaya says, 'Let's have everything outdoors, even the wedding ceremony. We can move it all to the bigger marquee if it rains.'

I go along. 'Yes, having a large marquee on the left of the *maṇḍapa* serves a purpose for those who want some protection from the elements. And the second marquee will be for food preparation and serving.'

We book the place there and then. As we wait for the manager to put together the digitised paperwork, I take out the photo of *Primavera* on my 6-inch smartphone. Kaya and Nadia's faces are blank like young children, but their eyes are scanning the details.

'Botticelli idealised the beauty of Venus, Clora and the three damsels. Such beauty can't exist; however, it shows that the mind is capable of scaling heights of beauty. It acts as a metaphor to seek the perfect.'

I get no response. Kaya and Nadia are both pointing at Clora's dress discussing the style of flowers printed on it.

We are in the car park, and I take one last look at the scenery. Kaya's the last one to sit in the car. Her face changes to a frown.

She says, 'Uncle, my worry is still about the weather in May. What if it's cold and wet? It will be unpleasant despite the marquee.'

'You sound like my sister, always worrying even when there's a plan in place.'

Kaya laughs. It's the same silly laugh she makes every time I poke fun at her mother.

I take my finger off the ignition button and move to my phone. I check on forecast trends in weather. The graphic shows May with a 10% chance of rain with an average temperature of 22°C at midday. This is so different from the time when I was growing up, when May could be a wipeout, and I didn't wear T-shirts until June.

'We will be fine in May. Anyhow, June is exam month for Nadia, and you know that July and August in the last few years have been too hot – all from climate change.'

Climate change is bad for the world, but it is now a blessing for us. I look at the photo of Nadia and Nabin on my car dashboard. They were three and six at the time. They are both jousting in a park.

'The children will love being outdoors and not trapped in a wedding hall. By my rough calculation, there are going to be almost thirty children under fifteen years old from our guest list of three hundred.'

Kaya's neck turns 90 degrees as we leave. As though imagining what her entrance will look like. I switch on the radio station that only plays pop hits from the last century. It heightens my mood, while Nadia and Kaya are in full flow discussing the wedding décor.

***

That night, the film *Groundhog Day* appears in my dreams. But the scenes have changed. It shows me doing the same job on the second floor forever, every day the same as the last. With iced buns on feature, as well as the dirty kitchenette. The old lady, together with the cleaning lady, appear as two-winged angels, each with a staff. They say together, 'Be attentive even to the mundane' and then add, 'It will help you break out of your spell.' One of my hands has a hanging handcuff on it and the other an iced bun. I am the sole human there; everywhere else are robots with shark heads meandering around me.

The dream is still vivid in the morning. I can't lather it out of my system in the shower. I can't find any washed T-shirts and wear my lavender shirt.

There is a new cleaner on her morning rounds. She ignores me. She is dusting the walls with her microfibre cloth, leaning up on her tiptoes to get to every spot.

She goes into the kitchenette. I am desperate for conversation and follow her in. She pushes the three dirty plates all on top of each other and then opens the tiny fridge. There is a smell of something gone off. She removes a plastic bowl of pasta. It's got mould on it. I am sure it's mine. Mona had insisted I take it to work and not waste money on expensive sandwiches. That was ten days ago.

'I am not sure who does this from your office.' She looks at my Rolex and then my shirt collar. 'I can see that you look after your things. It cannot be you, sir.'

I strike up a conversation with her. She talks about the dirty kitchen and then the weather; all the time hands are working. I sit on the small table. A plane is passing by. The sound tells me it's descending into City Airport.

I say, 'Nabin, my son, loves making paper plane models. I buy him as many Airfix kits as I can. It keeps him off his phone.'

She stops and sits on the chair opposite. She takes her dust cap off. Her eyes have the same look as the old woman in the park. She says, 'That's like my daughter. She prefers to use her hands and shies away from reading.' She leans back. She says, 'My daughter struggles a bit with grammar; she is dyslexic like me. But she is clever, I tell you. She is on grade four in piano. I also had the same problems, but nobody told me I had dyslexia till I was in my forties. That's why I failed my GCSEs.'

She gets up and checks her plastic watch. She picks up the sponge. An intelligent lady, trapped by circumstance. I wish Raff was around. I would have shared this story with him, and we would have pondered its meaning.

***

This winter is a complete blur: every weekday, there is a mix of iced buns, coffee, crisps and tedious music in the car. I haven't been invited for a single face-to-face interview. But I conclude from the stats that my CV is being read by plenty of people. The weekends are spent milling around the house, endlessly scrolling on social media and watching a big dose of crime series on Netflix. Mona listens to my endless moaning but has stopped giving me advice. The kids and I hardly talk unless they need something. The only change is that I try to take a bit more interest in work. It lifts me out of total misery, just being a bit more connected to my team. The thing that lifts me most is the preparation for Kaya's wedding and the visits to the Botticelli Discussion Group.

***

Our next meeting for the wedding preparation takes place on a cold February evening. Spring seems far away, and the heating is on full blast. The passage is cold from the door having to open and close several times. Kaya and I have prepared a checklist on our devices. With my regular calls with Kaya and Lekh, things have gathered pace and are now coming together.

Lekh starts with positive news, 'The Chair of the London Nepalese Buddhist Centre will officiate the wedding. They have agreed to our date and timings, but we need to pick them up and drop them back, as well as the two *bajrachāryas*.'

Last week, Lekh had arranged for his dad to talk to the senior *bajrachārya*.

He continues, 'And importantly the *bajrachārya* has given my dad assurance that there is nothing against our religion on our chosen dates.'

I do a thumbs up, my hand lifting to the ceiling.

Lekh's dad had rung me last week and asked many questions about the range of food and the style of decorations. I used to call Lekh's dad *kākā* when I was little but now just call him uncle.

I look at Lekh wanting his approval and say, 'You will be pleased to know that throughout the last few weeks, I have communicated our plan to *kākā* and some of our older cousins. We have listened to their expectations and will accommodate them where possible.'

I pause and look at Nabin and add, 'A great example of stakeholder management.'

Lekh gives me a glare – he always hated my management speak.

I ignore him and say, 'Catering is all arranged. We have gone for a Nepalese, Indian and British theme and will set up little stalls in the marquee.'

I get a half nod from my mum. She knows that Indian food has crept into everything, but that's the taste everyone wants now.

I continue, 'These will be replaced by dessert stalls in the evening. Also, the choir is sorted. We have found a wonderful group, courtesy of my work colleague, Emily.'

I have an image of the grounds in dark green and the welcoming marquees in the May sunshine.

Kaya speaks next. 'Uncle Lekh and I have found a supplier with crimson and white-coloured marquees to match the colours of Nepal. They will also provide all the furniture and decorations.'

∗∗∗

A few days later I get a text message from Peter: *If you are around, pop up between 5 and 5.30.* I sense a flame rising from the pit of my stomach. At 4:55 p.m. I take the lift to the top floor.

'How are you, Aman? I hope you have been staying out of trouble on the second floor.'

Peter is in his navy-blue suit. He has a light blue shirt and mint green tie to match. His room has a subtle smell of lavender. My workspace forever smells of food. I touch my face and play with the prickly stubble. My left sleeve has a glaring spot of dirt.

He gives me an update on DigiArt. I shake my knees. I wish he would stop the preamble and tell me why I am here.

He clears his throat. I stop shaking my knees. 'I am going to leave DigiArt next month. To be honest, I was planning my leave for a while. The pressures of work have put a strain on my health and a few things at home need sorting.'

I clench my fist and sit straight. I can hear my breathing. 'What's next for your career, Peter?'

'Well actually, I don't know. I am taking a six-month break, then I will decide after that. I have negotiated a payoff from the board and have enough to last a while.'

I am not sure why Peter is telling me so much. He holds his gaze at me and pauses. I sit up even straighter.

He says, 'I want to be honest with you, Aman. You are going to find it difficult to come back here. Tina is admired by the board and the company is limiting the number of new directors they take on. One non-exec, as you know, is not convinced about your abilities.' He shrugs and lifts his right shoulder. 'But you have sensed that. My best advice to you is to try and move on. I have spoken to the CEO. He can arrange to pay you three months of your old salary once you get another role.'

He looks towards the ceiling. 'I know that you and Joan have been in touch on a social level. I did send her a message to keep an eye out for opportunities for you. Stick with her, she has an interesting network.'

He is playing with his tie as if trying to get the words right. 'You were unfortunate, but in my experience that happens as often as lucky breaks. I know you will do well, Aman.'

He smiles. 'You can embellish your CV. And the CEO or I won't be challenging anything if I get a call from a recruiter or company.'

The smile disappears, his voice wavers and his shoulders lower. 'You just don't know; I may need to look you up for a job in the future.'

Till now all I have witnessed about Peter was his focus, and his ruthlessness. I want to reach out to Raff in his next life. To let him know he was spot on about Peter.

***

It's the 15th of April. At 7:30 a.m., it says 4°C on my car dashboard. I can't remember a cold April for many years. I pick up Larissa at Heathrow from her overnight flight from Port Louis. My sister has managed to get an agreement to work from London remotely while she helps Kaya with the wedding preparations. The terminal looks old; there is some grime on the walls. I took a flight to the Mediterranean with my parents three days after this building opened. At the time, it was considered state of the art.

My sister is unusually quiet as we join the M25. Last time I picked her up two years ago, we spent the whole journey arguing about whether a leader could ever change the culture inside an organisation. I need to steer any conversation well away from work.

Half an hour into our journey, it starts to drizzle. There is a smell of dampness in the car. She asks for the heating to be put on higher.

'Are you sure the outdoors will work for Kaya's wedding, Aman? A month to go. What if it rains heavily? British weather is so unpredictable.'

I say, 'We discussed all this with the family already. And you know we have contingency plans in place. Anyway, I know more about risk management than you. The long-range forecast predicts warm weather in May. Of course we'll have more certainty two weeks beforehand. We have two large marquees just in case.'

She speaks slowly in a single pitch, 'I feel we should book a large hall as a back-up. I am not convinced about the weather being right for the outdoor wedding.'

My foot finds itself pushing the accelerator. I say, 'That's strange coming from you. You always went on about how risk needs to be considered alongside opportunity. I thought that's why you went to Mauritius.'

The peace between my sister and I always lasts a short while. From my teenage years, we'd always have some form of argument every week. We interrupt each other until I drop her at my mum's house. I am glad she is not staying with me. The wedding is just five weeks away.

CHAPTER 9

THE BIG DAY

———

Three weeks later, I get my first job interview. The office is in a bog-standard building typical for medium-sized technology companies. The tiny room has a faint whiff of detergent, and the air is stale.

The director arrives ten minutes late, doesn't apologise, and checks his phone twice. Both times, it is while I am speaking. He is seven years younger than me. I know that from LinkedIn. He reminds me of Louis. A rounded nose but with deep-set piercing eyes. He must have been to his hairdresser yesterday. He scans my CV back and forth on his iPad. I want to tell him, *You could have read it before the interview.* I give him some stock answers to his standard questions on Cloud technology.

At the end, he looks at his watch; I'm certain it's the updated Breitling. He taps his watch and asks me if I have any questions.

'What's the company culture like?'

His voice is like one of those AI-generated marketing ads. 'We move fast and believe in delivering value by unleashing our people's talent.'

He seems to believe in what he is saying, pausing through every point in his sentence. He gazes at me, wanting me to react. I nod at double speed, but my left hand is being squeezed by my thighs under the table.

Less than a minute after I leave the building, I get a call from the recruiter. I don't answer. I need to get away from the building as fast as possible.

I expected a flood of calls from recruiters, like when I was last looking for a job three years ago. My tally to date is three. There is plenty of demand for work in my field; I get many alerts on my job app. But they all want skills in product creation or implementing the latest technology. I shake my head. I want to call Raff on my car phone and shout, *The whole market is wrong. The focus should be on joined-up thinking, not the fads.*

The first thing I do back in my office is to find the ground-floor toilet cubicle, making sure there is no-one else around. I stamp my feet, cover my eyes with my hands and whisper, '*Pāgal, pāgal, pāgal.*'

At DigiArt, I put great emphasis on joining things up, but now everyone wants things done fast. Worse than that, ageism has crept in. Five years' experience is now enough for a senior role.

In some vain hope, I shuffle on the toilet seat and look at another role on offer. I check the company's Technology Director's details on LinkedIn. His photo makes him look ten years younger than me. His profile shows achievement after achievement, and he has tagged global companies to his name. How can I compete against this? Either I'll work for some youngster who wants me to follow his milestones, or I'll spend an eternity on the second floor until some AI takes over my job.

***

Two weeks before the wedding, we have our final meeting at my home.

Precisely at 8 p.m., I hear noise from outside the front door. By my porch, Lekh and the neighbour's eight-year-old boy are having a conversation.

The cornflower buds by the hedge outside my house are sprouting. On two buds, I can see the purple colour emerging.

I hear Lekh saying, 'So, what are you doing with those cans?'

The boy says, 'I like throwing them and hearing the different sounds they make. I will show you.'

He throws an empty can onto the other and laughs at the clinking sound. Lekh does his characteristic blink and gives him a big thumbs up. The boy ignores my presence. He looks up at my pine tree from the fence in my garden. He holds his hand to his ear. I can hear birds twittering.

He points and says, 'That's a robin and a blackbird. Looks like they are talking to each other. My dad says they don't like artificial light from humans.'

The boy and Lekh laugh in the same rhythm despite their age gap.

In the living room, Lekh says, 'What an amazing boy. They say some kids are sound sensitive, they pick up timbre and pitch immediately. As if the structure is already something they are born with.' He looks at the Buddha statue on the piano.

He says, 'That boy's karma from his past life allows him to experience strong senses.'

I have two emotions: guilt and happiness. All this time, the young boy wasn't intentionally creating a mess in my garden. And that's why he liked kicking my tyre wheels.

My sister arrives a few minutes later with my mum. She is dressed in a scarf, an elegant blue dress and her winter jacket. My mum is in tow with a thick cream jacket with collar padding. She has a traditional woven basket called a *dōkō*. Lekh bows to my mum and gives a high five and then a tight hug to my sister.

'I have made some *yōmārī* for everyone.'

Mum passes the basket to Mona as naturally as a handshake.

Mona takes out the banana leaves covering the dumplings from the bamboo bottom of the basket.

Lekh's nostrils are wide.

He says, 'I smell the cinnamon. At home, we make it with rice flour and molasses, but it looks like you have made these with a mix of different flours.'

My mum turns towards me, but her eyes are on Lekh.

'I have filled the rice and maize dough with chocolate and these two with coconut. Aman likes the chocolate ones. Lekh *chhōrā*, I remember you like coconut.'

I had no idea how *yōmārī* were made, just that they were always in plentiful supply growing up, particularly when Lekh came round.

My sister's cheeks are flushing, and her shoulders are wide. From what I know, she has already had several arguments with Kaya since she arrived. But she loves the detailed plans for the outdoor wedding.

Kaya's dad is on the big screen; his slim body hardly occupies any space. I can make out more bits of the white swirl of the sea behind him, even though it is almost midnight in Mauritius. He will fly in next week and leave three days after the wedding. I look at Kaya. She loves being in this house. At this moment, I must feel more like a dad to Kaya than the man in Mauritius.

I can feel the sensation of my breath on my top lip as we go around getting updates. Lekh and I have at least one thing in common: we plan things well in advance. He is scrolling through his list, and I have mine. Kaya has a printout of menus, dress pictures and the venue photos on the floor. She is the only person I know who has a printer at home. Even when she was young, she preferred old-fashioned felt tip pens and paper – not the digital drawing pad.

I say, 'A few details still. We need to agree on the decorative pieces, including the ornaments on the outdoor seating tables. They need to blend with the greenery. And to confirm the final order of events and the timing arrangements with the caterers. But first we need to nail down the remaining starters. Are we agreed with potatoes and pea samosas and *chānā chatpāt*?'

Lekh blinks like he is auditing my work.

He says, 'We – I would have preferred *barā*. Aman, you know that. It used to be a must at weddings, but I understand we want to be eclectic.'

Our eclectic wedding has a choir, a nice variety of dishes for food, the English country grounds and a traditional ceremony with two *bajrachāryas*. Plus a vintage car and an evening disco to finish. I wish Raff was here to witness the work put in. I learnt so much from him about joining things up.

Kaya nudges Lekh's foot. He shuffles; his arms are still half-folded.

He says, 'We have done well. The wedding is going to be remembered for a long time. It embraces modern and traditional elements for Kaya and Remi. Our guests will not be upset.' He looks at Kaya, then me. He says, 'Grandad would be proud of us. If he was here, he would have loved that we involved the whole family.'

I cross my legs. I want to grumble about Lekh's praise, but I like it. Instead, I say, 'Now, let's think about what could go wrong. First, though, let's get the weather out of the way.' I wave my phone. 'I have the forecast from the Met Office that predicts a temperature of 21°C and little chance of rain.'

My sister interrupts, 'If that is the case, then nothing else will go wrong; we should be positive and visualise that all will be good.'

I want to shake my head. That was the opposite of her concern only two weeks ago.

'Things go wrong in our complex world, and we need to plan for all eventualities. Let's all pair up and come up with as many things as possible.'

At the end, we have thirteen risks, all numbered on my iPad.

These include the possibility that Kaya's dress rips, guests have a fight or a sudden illness occurs. For each potential risk, a remedial action is suggested just in case. Everyone is nodding apart from Larissa. She has a frown. I start my next point.

But she interrupts, 'Do we need to do this? I am sure nothing is going to go wrong. We have thought of everything.'

My teeth are biting. I say, 'Life can be unpredictable. If shit happens, we will meet, apart from Kaya and Nadia of course, in the kitchen in the abbey to make decisions.'

Nadia and Nabin start giggling.

My mum and Lekh both turn their heads away from me. They are looking at the Buddha bust on the piano.

I want to say to them, *Shit is such a common word.*

***

In these last two weeks, I have good gaps when I am not worrying about my work status. My mind doesn't race as much. Everyone at work is no longer a possible enemy.

In the mornings, I get on top of the mundane jobs: the service reports, marking up the PDFs. In the afternoons, at 3 p.m., I slip into an empty meeting room. I make calls to check up on wedding suppliers, managing RSVPs and sometimes coaxing elderly relatives to make the trip. I call Lekh several times for assurance. Whatever happens to our relationship after the wedding, for the next two weeks we need to be aligned. My Cloud planning board – full of tasks, documents, calendar entries – is getting bigger. No-one sitting around me mentions my change of attitude.

My boss spent our last meeting asking for advice in skills matching for a new role he wants to advertise. He didn't mention the quality of my work once.

The evening before the wedding, my mind scans for every possible thing I could have forgotten.

I call Lekh just before midnight. 'Have you checked that the *bajrachāryas* will arrive on time? You have already fixed their transportation, right?'

His calm voice releases the tightness in my shoulder.

At night, I dream about the wedding. I can see Kaya and Remi at the *maṇḍapa*, my distant relatives in Nepal on video, the *bajrachāryas* laughing and tasty food arranged. I see a picture of me dressed as a pilot on a runway. The plane belly is being loaded with wedding ornaments, green grass and *chānā chatpāt*. Kaya and Remi are sitting at the front with me. I turn around and every seat on the plane is full.

Just before 5 a.m., I am wide awake and am up in a flash. I switch on my phone and look at my checklist. Mona is snoring in a low hum next to me. By 6 a.m., the kitchen is full of sunrays adding to the excitement as the kids munch into the ready-made croissants. It feels exactly the same as when we first moved into the house and huddled in the kitchen every morning, to get the kids' rucksacks ready for primary school.

The doorbell rings at 6:30 a.m.; Larissa arrives with her hairdresser in tow. I notice John's bedroom curtain move. When Larissa and I were little, the neighbours would look out of their window, to admire my mum in her *sārī*.

My sister smells of sharp citrus and sandalwood, triggering in my mind a montage of every family wedding that I have ever been to.

At 7:30 a.m., Mona, Nabin and I leave our home. Nadia stands on the doorstep and says, 'Kaya arrives here in fifteen minutes, Dad. You look relaxed. It's going to be an amazing wedding. See you in four hours.'

Kaya has a long four hours to get ready, but I can sense beads of sweat on my forehead already.

When we arrive at Bushey Abbey, the large marquee is already up. I count the number of cumulus clouds out loud. There are seven. Nabin laughs at my counting. As we walk on the grass to the planned atrium, I hum *oṃ maṇi padme hūṃ*. Grandad used to make me recite this mantra on certain days of the month. Mona picks up the melody and sings it out loud.

By 9:30 a.m., we have all three hundred seats facing the front of the *maṇḍapa* and around 70% of decorations in place. Mona, Nabin, Lekh and his family, my sister and her husband, Sunita plus Kaya's and Remi's three friends are all there. Silently working as per our plan. We don't say much, yet I feel connected with our common purpose.

The chairs are in some sort of symmetry across the ground. I sit down and catch my breath. It's the first time I gaze at the grounds from end to end. They look phenomenal, the grass finely cut and dark green. On my right are the cornflowers in bloom; on my left, three giant oak trees provide a shadow onto the grounds. The photographer is due to arrive soon. I reach out to my phone and check the forecast again. The chance of rain remains at 7%.

I take a last glance in the changing room mirror. Mona chose the indigo tie. My three-button suit, with my pink shirt, blends well.

Nabin appears a few minutes later. He looks older and more handsome in his blue suit, also with a bright blue tie. Twenty minutes pass and everyone is on the lawn, transformed from our casual gear apart from my sister. It takes me a minute to spot Mona in a green, flowery *sārī*. Her make-up brings out the features I like: her round face and her oval eyes. She comes up next to me and pats my backside. I nudge her shoulder. She gives me the same look she gave me on our wedding day. Lekh has a crisp white shirt and a pink tie. The photographer has already started. He is snapping all the décor, before the guests fill the space.

One of our innovations for connection is a video link of the wedding to our cousins in Nepal and Remi's cousins who are spread throughout France. My estimate is that fifty will be watching. Twelve have already connected, well before the official time. As more Nepalese cousins sign in, I can see that almost all are in wedding attire. The men are in *tapālan* or lengthy shirts and the women in *sārīs*. A few have banners with words in Devanagari script, surrounded by painted purple peacock feathers.

I ask Lekh what it says.

He shakes his head and laughs. 'It's what you'd expect, Aman. It says *Bhīn-Īhipā* which means Auspicious Wedding.'

The waiting team look like grown-up schoolchildren – in black trousers and cream shirts. The red and white cut glasses are arranged on the table in a diagonal pattern by the caterers. It is the same way Grandad had arranged them for my wedding, but that was with plastic cups. The sound of ginger being shredded is emanating from the food marquee. I check my watch. 11 a.m. Kaya will arrive at midday. Food served from 2 p.m. onwards. The smell of ginger hits my nose. I could be in Kathmandu ...

In front of the 4-foot-tall shrine of Buddha are long thin candles and four lotus flowers. Nadia told me they have been grown in a greenhouse in the UK. The candles will be lit by the couple with the sandalwood incense sticks. This will be part of the ceremony – seeking blessing from the Buddha. After that, Kaya and Remi will recite the three holy mantras. Someone shouts my name. I move towards the *maṇḍapa*. An old lady, five feet tall, is there in an immaculate green *sārī*. She is wearing golden earrings, one bangle in each hand and little make-up. She is familiar.

Then it hits me. It's the officiant from the *Bāhā*, the same one who administered my wedding. I am expecting a face of wrinkles but can't find any.

Mona and I had made a pledge to her on our wedding day to visit the *Bāhā* frequently. I shake hands and then bow to her. I act like I have never met her.

She says, 'Mr Pradhan, I have been through the rituals and the order of events.' She holds up the conch shell. She says, 'I like the *śankha*. I think I have seen this design, with the Buddha carved on it with a grey outline. Perhaps at another family wedding?'

My grandad had said that the shell signified purity and Buddha's teachings.

Ten minutes later, the two *bajrachāryas* arrive. They are half an hour early, chaperoned by Lekh and his dad. The atmosphere becomes more serene. Lekh sits them right in front on the two decorated seats with embossed gold covers.

Almost all our side of the family in Nepal have joined half an hour before the time ... Many have gathered outside with their devices in what looks like an open field. The camera is on the *bajrachāryas,* who get up, curious to see who is on the screen. They start talking in Nepalbhasa. Everyone unmutes, there is a jumble of noise and bowing. In the end, they give up having a conversation. The *bajrachāryas* just wave.

At 11:40 a.m., I get a call from Nadia. My heart misses a beat. We had agreed to use phone calls for urgent matters. I wander to the nearest oak tree, away from the growing crowd. I can hear her breath.

She shouts, 'Dad, the Regent Vintage car has had a minor crash coming to us and the front part is in bad shape. It is drivable but looks bad – the steel bumper has fallen off. The limousine company is trying to get another car. I am trying my best to keep Kaya calm.'

This Regent car was meant to drive through the grounds in full view before coming right up to the top marquee, an essential part of the wedding delight. A banged-up car would be out of the question.

The veins on my wrist are throbbing, but my mind is not troubled. My intuition was expecting something to go wrong. I send out a message verbally via Nabin and get our team into a huddle in the estate kitchen. I see my sister in her *sārī* for the first time. It's crimson with intricate swirling shapes embossed in pink and green. But all the colour has gone from Larissa's face.

'The wedding is going to start late; an hour – maybe two.'

Larissa looks at me like it's my fault. 'What will the *bajrachāryas* and guests think of our family?!'

All eyes are on me. I cough. Nabin hands me a crystal glass with fresh orange juice.

I hear a ping from my phone: *Dad. Have arranged a car – a Viscount – but it is 30 miles away* 😟. *Will take at least an hour to arrive and we will have to swap the decorations. Kaya says you need to delay things there.*

I read out the message. I hear heels tapping and fingers clicking. I want to take my tie off. Nabin comes and stands closer to me. He is less of a boy in his three-piece. His buttons are all still done up.

'Dad, why don't we do the choir as a warm-up, before Kaya arrives?'

The commotion dies. There is a five-second silence and then a few nods around the room. We agree to get the choir to entertain the guests – but more importantly, open the food marquee for canapés straight away.

Mona adds, 'Let's spend this time introducing both sides of the family to each other. Do you remember how your grandad said this was so important? A wedding is a joining of families, not only the bride and groom.'

Lekh nods at double speed. I half clench my fist. Why didn't I say that? One reason not to use a wedding planner is that they have no experience of family dynamics. Grandad told me once in Nepal-bhasa, 'A wedding is not a tactical process.'

Everyone moves back outside. Mona comes up to me and touches my cheek.

'Your face is all screwed up. What will be will be. Just enjoy yourself as well. Grandad would be proud of you today. Don't let your sister upset you.'

Under the guidance of Nabin, we move chairs towards the lake one hundred metres away. The caterers and some guests help without asking. We make six circles of ten seats. People mingle and extend themselves onto the grounds.

The photographer follows us as we do our improvised work. He is bending, moving and squatting while taking pictures of our motion.

Ten minutes later, Nabin has gathered eight children. He has a football in his hand. His jacket is off and lying on the grass.

Lekh and I find Remi's cousin, Jai. The three of us start mingling with the ever-growing number of guests. There must be one hundred and fifty people here now. I meet one doctor, an architect, a postmaster, two traders and three people working in supermarkets. Many are from all around the country, including Cardigan, Edinburgh and Chichester, places I have not been to. But a majority are from London or near Aldershot.

My feet are hurting. Lekh and I find two spare chairs in a corner away from the heart of the crowd. Lekh moves his left hand in an arc, 'Look at all those people enjoying themselves. I had a brilliant chinwag with Remi's brother, what a wonderful family.' I feel more elated than any holiday I have taken. What's more, with Lekh by my side, all the pressure has gone.

There is a howl of laughter from my left as my two sets of cousins laugh at a joke. George would love this mingling. I wish I had invited him. My grandad told me, even the shyest people, once prompted, like to make connections.

The *bajrachāryas* are considered our important guests. Lekh and I enter the food tent. The three serving tables are laid out in a kind of triangle. We wanted a blend of East and West. On my right is *mōmō*, a kind of dumpling, freshly steamed. In front of me, mini Indian samosas with a dark green coriander and thick brown tamarind chutney, and next to it the *chānā chatpāt*. And on my left, pea, potato and pesto croquettes. The Indian samosas were never my choice, but now they have become part of Nepali food. We load the two large ceramic plates for the *bajrachāryas* until there is no space.

Lekh leads me to the *bajrachāryas*. He reminds me to address them as *guru-jū*. I stand by his side. He informs them of the delayed ceremony after presenting the plates. The eldest *guru-jū*'s face is unchanged. His body, largely still, moves slightly to his right. He nods a few seconds later and goes back to the conversation he is having with Lekh's dad.

Seeing all the food suddenly makes my gut juices kick-start. Once, during a distant relative's wedding, Dad was hungry. On arrival, we all headed directly to the buffet; Mum protested and then tagged along with us. Only after an hour of eating and social-ising did we go find the newlywed couple and hand over the card and gift.

Lekh compiles a dish of starters and takes it near the camera to show our virtual visitors. Most faces come closer to the screen. A few are pointing as Lekh explains the menu. Two virtual guests are taking photos of their screen.

Lekh and I share his dish. He dips his samosa into both the tamarind and coriander chutney. That makes no sense. Mum always insisted when we were growing up that we dip into only a single chutney for each samosa. Lekh laughs when I remind him of his slip-up.

'I think that depends on individual preference, Aman, nothing to do with ancient ways.'

The choir is standing in a tight circle finishing their food up. Their leader comes towards me.

He gives me a thumbs up. 'The choir are almost ready.'

He adds, 'We all love the *mōmō*.' His dish is empty; I take it off him and arrange a refill.

Once the choir starts, a small crowd gathers, everyone with a plate of food. The samosas seem to be the most popular. By the right of the lake, a seven-year-old girl in a *hākū patāsī* is flying a frisbee with her pals. Nadia had a *hākū patāsī* when she was little and had ripped it on her first outing. On the left-hand side two makeshift goals, made of children's jackets, mark the perimeter. The football they are kicking has streaks of grass stains on it.

Remi is surrounded by people, almost all from our side of the family. On his right is the big screen. He is reading the messages and waving to the people on screen. I have never seen him like this. Maybe he knows all the attention on him will disappear when Kaya arrives. I open the chat function on the screen. Someone has written in English: *With the pale skin, he looks Bhutanese.* Underneath are responses in emojis. I want to delete the comments. Remi is pointing to them and laughing.

On the top right, I see Grandad. I feel I am back in the 90s. Is Grandad back? I go closer to the screen. Then it hits me, it's my great-uncle looking much older than when I talked to him about two years ago. He waves and unmutes. His blue and white chequered Nepalese *ṭōpī* is prominent. He must be near ninety now. After my grandad died, I started calling him *Hajurābubā*.

Hajurābubā says slowly in broken English, rather than Nepalbhasa, 'Aman, boy, we all happy. Your *ājā* wrote a special letter to me. I still have it. He said, Aman will follow all tradition.'

I like that there are so many different ways of saying grandad.

He removes his *ṭōpī* and waves it. 'You are doing job in the *Prem Bibāha*. Good, good.' He waves his palm, which is covering his camera.

I want to hold his hand. The creases on the top of his palm look just like my grandad's.

Hajurābubā says in perfect pronunciation, 'Prem Bibāha. Love marriage in Nepali, in case you didn't know.'

I wish I knew more than basic Nepali Mum had taught me.

Emily is by my side. She is my only work friend and got on the wedding invite list on the grounds that she has helped with the planning. As my grandad would say, it's not the full truth but neither a lie.

I explain the situation. She gives me a tap on my shoulder.

'Good to see you are going with the flow.'

At 12:23 p.m., I get a text from Nadia: *The replacement car is here, we are putting the decorations on the front. All cool Dad, Kaya has calmed down* 😬.

At 1:30 p.m., the automated gates at the top open. A crimson Viscount drives in. The driver has a black peak cap. The car must be rolling in first gear. Kaya and Nadia are at the back and Kaya's friend in front. It takes five minutes to come down the driveway. The choir restarts. The videographer is scrambling around the moving car. The youngest kids have disposed of their frisbee. They are running behind the car. About one hundred phones are pointing to the Viscount. The hum of the choir resonates with the rhythm of the car engine, interrupted by the cry from a baby.

Kaya puts her left foot out of the car to reveal her hand-stitched *sārī*. It's red and green, with hints of white and blue on its edges. She looks like a cross between Venus from *Primavera,* the rich lady from the *Arnolfini* painting and the way my sister looked at her wedding. She has Nadia on her left and her friend on her right. Their cheeks are rosy. Kaya pauses for photos, moving her head from right to left, without any hesitation.

I see the glow on her face as she walks towards the wedding *maṇḍapa*, our ornate pavilion adorned with flowing cloth drapes, delicate flower garlands and flickering lights, all under the open sky. Her dad is now by her left. Remi is standing on the right side of the *maṇḍapa*. She gives him a fast glance and then moves her eyes in sync with the *guru-jū*. They both light the candles and incense sticks. This starts the ceremony. I want to loosen my tie. The officiant asks for silence during the process. Half the people ignore it. It's the people from our side of the family. I want to stand up and ask them to be quiet. Instead, Lekh and I look at each other and shake our heads. We won't be able to stop the chatting. The background noise rises. Many of Kaya and Remi's friends are taking photos, their lips are sealed, but they are not still.

Lekh and I help two elderly guests who decide in the middle of the ceremony that they want to sit next to each other. My mind is running with all the tasks yet to do. I have already resigned myself to watching the wedding properly on replay a few days later. The bit about the vows comes out clearly through the speaker. The officiant has the translation from the text in her hand. She says, 'And the duty of the wife is to protect savings and invest earnings.'

Mona taps my thigh and whispers 'Ha.'

The *bajrachāryas* emanate a stillness that calms me despite the chatting all around. The minute they stand to give blessings, I know the main ceremony is nearly over and turn round to peek at the food marquee.

Kaya's dad delivers a gushing speech, all about Kaya's happy childhood, but is in tears three minutes in.

Lekh's dad is next up. As Kaya's maternal great-uncle, he has a special part. He says a few words in English interwoven with Nepal-bhasa and Nepali about our roots, the pains of growing up in this country and some wonderful things about his new grandnephew.

He finishes in English, 'The joining of East and West has been continuous over the last one hundred years. Kaya is part of that join; may she preserve both traditions and heritages.'

Some of my family members stand up and clap.

According to custom, the bride and groom say nothing at the wedding. After all they are only part of the backdrop of a family occasion.

But Kaya is up. After thanking both sets of parents, she looks at me, her face as bright as Botticelli's *Venus*. 'Mona *maijū* and Aman *māmā* have been at the centre of planning this wedding. I grew up with them and Nadia and Nabin. My parents are, of course, there for me. But my outlet when my parents ... my parents got me frustrated was to hang around at *māmā* and *maijū*.'

Nadia starts giggling.

Kaya looks at Lekh in the same way she looked at me. 'I want to thank Lekh *māmā* for his guidance and wisdom.'

Kaya's speech was never in our plan. My sister has a frown, which changes to a forced smile. Remi stands up and then every single person is up, three hundred people all staring at Mona, Lekh and me. I get up. The beating sound elates me. Every single person on the screen is clapping or waving. Mona pats my thigh the moment I sit down.

The last time this happened was at the Cloud Awards two years ago, where two hundred people were present. The pleasure from that had lasted only for a week.

My stomach clenches and feels like stone. What will I do tomorrow? I have a picture of sitting at my desk on the second floor, with the smell from the filthy kitchenette. Sweat is all over my forehead.

Five minutes later, I mumble an excuse to Mona and wander to the food marquee. I loosen my tie and unhook the top button ...

The caterers all have their heads down and don't acknowledge me. I wander round to their cooking space. It has been curtained off. We want the food to be as fresh as possible, but without lengthy queues. The first lot of *tarkārī* and the eggplant *bhūtwā* are all ready and onto the chafing plates. The vegetable rice is pre-prepared. There is a pile of eighty *purīs* on a large steel plate and another ten being cooked in the *karaī*. There is a man rolling out the *purī* dough into 12 cm circles. At the bottom of the tent is a portable oven. The prepared pizzas are by its side, ready to be baked.

Twenty minutes later there is a long queue. There is always one at Nepalese weddings. Lekh and I run around helping any elderly with their plates or explaining ingredients. I was hungry an hour ago – now I have no appetite.

Lekh's dad comes to me. 'Aman *chhōrā*, please eat something. People will take care of themselves.' He raises his eyebrows. 'You remind me of my dad, keeping the oil of happiness flowing.'

I agree, if Grandad was here, he would love watching guests take pleasure from food.

I opt to have the *ālū-kāulī tarkārī* with *purī*. Lekh gestures for me to sit next to him. We don't exchange a word but talk to guests who come to chat with us. I can't remember the last time we shared a meal together. One of my cousins, a few years younger than my dad, comes towards me. I can't recall his name. I want to open the guest list to find out, but that would be rude.

'Hey Aman. This reminds me of your wedding. It was amazing as well. Only thing was that it was in the function hall, and it got so hot inside.'

I find it funny when older people from Nepal say *hot* when they mean *warm*. The music changes to 'Show Me Love' by Robin S.

He laughs, 'The music from the 80s and 90s has made a revival. Did they play that one at your wedding?'

I can't remember, I want to ask Mona, but nod anyway.

His smile fades. 'Your dad would have been proud to be here. He would have been dancing like your grandad. He worked so hard, Aman, with all that travelling. It's a pity he is not here to enjoy this moment. Sad, he died so young.'

I know he died so young. I want to put my hands over my eyes. Instead, I say, 'Your plate is nearly empty; shall I get some hot samosas?'

He gets up and taps me twice on my shoulder.

I check the schedule on my phone. Two more items remain for the evening. The troupe to do the *maruṇī* dance at 6 p.m., followed by dessert. The last event will be the disco, which starts at 8:30 p.m.

At 11 p.m. Kaya and Remi are still dancing. Kaya is full of a kind of morning energy. I am exhausted. There is one person still connected from Nepal on Zoom. It's 3:45 a.m. in Kathmandu, yet he is moving side to side with the beat.

The disco stops at 11:30 p.m. It was part of the booking arrangement, to limit 'noise pollution.' There are about seventy people left. Lekh is sipping mint tea and biting into a coconut biscuit. The food marquee is almost dismantled. Two vans are being filled with wedding décor. They will find themselves at another celebration next weekend. I look up. The sky is dark, a few clouds and a half moon. With the floodlights, I can see the silhouette of the oak trees forty metres away. The bushes and shrubbery are all dark green. One star is on its own just above the trees.

Jai, Remi's cousin, comes and pulls his chair close to mine. I am beginning to like this young man. He follows my eyes. He says, 'That's Mars, not a star.'

I am not so sure.

He pulls out his phone and shows me. 'It says, Mars is a planet visible in May.' He says, 'Ha' loudly and continues, 'They say it is the ruler of business and communication.' He taps his phone and says, 'And trickery.'

I laugh out loud. 'The only Mars I know for sure is the picture of *Mars and Venus* from the Renaissance.'

Jai keeps looking at Mars. 'I hear that you are in the world of digitising art. Remi told me a little about what you do, and I had a look at your LinkedIn profile during dinner. Well, I work in recruitment for start-ups, and we are searching for a Commercial and Product Director.' He pushes his business card towards me.

My brain goes numb. Why do I need to be reminded of work? I want to tell him to go away. Instead, I look up at Mars, and what my grandad told me comes up in a flash. 'Do you know we call that planet Mars *Mangal* in Nepalbhasa? It symbolises action and strength.'

***

Two days later, we attend a reception lunch. Remi, or perhaps his parents, have organised an event planner to put everything in place. It's easy to spot the wedding planner; she is wearing bright blue jeans and a black top. She doesn't stand still and has an iPad, which her eyes are glued to. Her body is alert, her face is smiling but she has no warmth. She is like an alien intruder, as far as I am concerned.

The venue is the Hertford Hotel, with one hundred and fifty people in attendance. In the corner are the newlyweds. Kaya is in a cream dress while Remi has a three-piece suit. I keep one eye on the wedding planner as I mingle. The planner is scrolling on her iPad and looking at us like we are the cast of some play.

Uncle starts talking to me, about the wedding day and who he met. I am barely listening.

Lekh interrupts his dad and comes up to me and says in my ear, 'I know what you are thinking: *Hajurābubā* would have laughed at having a wedding planner. You can't outsource your family, he would say.'

I chortle and say, 'Does she have any sense of who is who, family dynamics or even improvisation of plans?'

Mona is disturbed by our giggling. She comes right up and pinches my bicep. 'Stop looking at that pretty woman; you are ignoring what *kākā* is saying.'

I turn my back to the planner and reconnect with my uncle. But all I want to do is check whether she has joined everything up.

We are ushered into the refurbished ballroom, our large circular table close to Kaya and Remi's. The tables are laden with shining silver. I spend all my time talking to Lekh.

I go over the wedding day and all the incidents we observed. We laugh and grimace together, like we did during our teenage years. He is playing with his white napkin. He opens the napkin, attempts to make some origami shapes, and then unfolds it again completely.

He leans to me and says, 'Let's forget about the silly family issue between our dads. It was their dispute, not ours. Why spoil it for our children; they had a wonderful time at the wedding together.'

I want to let Lekh know the reason for my dad's anger.

Remi's dad says some nice but forgetful words about Kaya. The three-piece band starts their song. It calms me. Everyone on our table starts humming to 'What a Wonderful World' by Louis Armstrong. Why couldn't they use a different song? I have heard this one so many times at weddings. Yet, I hum as well and fold my napkin into smaller triangles. Lekh is looking away from me.

'Agreed,' I respond.

He turns his eyes to me, and I give him a fist bump.

Grandad made me watch Bollywood films from the 70s and 80s when I was between seven and eleven. The standard theme was two brothers at loggerheads or sometimes separated at birth. A common enemy is encountered, which unites them. It always ended with recon-ciliation. And of course, dispersed through the film would be songs and dances.

The next song picks up the beat with the bass drum more in action. I want them to change the tune to *'Resham Firirī,'* tie napkins to the end of my fingers and dance with Lekh. We used to do this without any coordination, waving our arms like crazy and trying to copy Larissa's hip movements. I whisper my thoughts to Lekh, who whispers to his wife on his right. Larissa is looking at us from the head table. She laughs as we wave our hands in the air.

***

I drop my sister at the airport ten days later. It's 6:15 a.m., and the sun is already visible, 30% above the horizon. My brother-in-law departed last week due to his work schedule.

The business class check-in has no queue. Minutes later, we go up two floors to the café and find two seats. Through the large window, I see the back part of an Air Mauritius plane. I wanted to get a large cappuccino, but I have a mint tea. I look at the corridor. Busy executives are moving – there is not a second to waste. Most have an expensive hard-cover roll-on suitcase, a laptop bag and a phone in hand. Each one in their own world.

I turn to my sister who is sipping the sugar-laden coffee, her gaze on the table. I point to the plane. It has the silhouette of a red bird on its frame.

I say, 'Thought it might have the famous dodo, but that would be worrying, having a bird that can't fly.'

I start laughing and close my eyes, waiting for my sister to join in. There is no response.

'What's the matter?' I say. 'Did I do something wrong at the wedding, or are you tired?'

She takes a sip and then places her mug between us. 'I may lose my job and be made redundant. The company I work for has a new leader and he says the culture is outdated.'

Her voice grows louder.

'I already feel threatened about my process of working. They want young dynamic people, not hard-working professionals. I have spent my whole working life getting to this position. A six-month payoff is no substitute. It's going to be impossible to get a similar position unless I move back to the UK. And I don't want to come back to this country; I hate your winter.'

She clinks the mug with her wedding ring and looks at the sky. 'Maybe I am like the dodo, going extinct. You always end up doing better than me.'

I check left to see if our neighbours are eavesdropping. The people next to us are in an animated conversation, about some telecoms deal.

I speak in a soft tone, 'You're looking at things the wrong way and being negative.'

I want to talk about what I have been through at DigiArt, but I decide not to. If I start talking, everything might spill out too quickly.

'You are my big sister, and I admire you regardless of your work status.'

She takes hold of her mug. I press my lips together. She changes the subject and talks about the wedding and the gossip on our cousins. The gate announcement is up on the large screen.

I walk her up to the entrance of passport control. I want to blurt out all my troubles.

She gives me a hug, tight but quick. A minute later, she is on the other side of the barrier. She waves her passport at me. Her smartphone is already out of her bag.

On the way back home from the airport, on the A4, I drive well under the speed limit. I already told my boss I'd arrive late. The heavy A380 is coming towards me. Its wheels are down, and its huge fuselage casts a shadow across the whole field in front of me. Frankly, I have nothing to look forward to. My mirror shows a glimpse of the runway behind. I have nowhere to land, nothing to aim towards. On my worklist today is to review a statistical report and check some logs. It's no different to the work I did after I graduated. I am a prisoner on the second floor and can't seem to find a way to escape to something better.

That night, my grandad appears in my dreams. His cheeks are flush, and his gaze is on my nose. He points at me and speaks for a minute. I reach out to him, and he holds three of my fingers. He has the blue-headed statue of the Buddha in his other hand. In the morning, I wake up and can't remember a single word. But Grandad said a lot.

The next morning, at the crossroads, there is a large advert on a billboard. It is a Middle East airline with its business-class cabin. The strapline is *Dazzling Cabins, Luxurious Destinations.*

The picture has seats that are wide enough to fit two normal people, Bose headphones dangling from the headrest. And virtual windows with clouds and greenery outside. I take the next left turn and stop on the double yellow line and put my hazard lights on. I open the notes app and write. My grandad's words from last night appear like a film reel: *Difficult roads often lead to beautiful destinations.*

He had pointed to the blue-headed Buddha and said, *Every morning we are born again. What we do today matters most. Say yes sometimes.* He'd grasped my fingers tighter and then let go.

Just before midday, I mull over which sandwich to buy. I used to like the cress, spinach and pickle sandwich, but now find it boring. My mobile phone rings.

It's Louis. 'Tina is back, boss. She has sent me a thank you note. She said she was impressed with my management of the area and that I had kept the show moving. Cheers for your coaching and support all the time I have known you.'

He pauses. I can hear him take a deep breath. 'I am still using many of the tools you have taught me. Tina is struggling with how to get the team to be better at decision-making. Can I ask her to contact you?'

I say 'Yes' instantly. I want to add, *I was coaching the team on decision-making and problem-solving tools, but the organisation sacked me.*

After lunch, I don't wait for Tina and send her a note. She responds on text with: *Great, thank you. Sending the invite now* 👍.

***

Five days later I step into the large fourth-floor meeting room. It feels like I have never left. My depression has vanished.

I pace the front; all eyes are on me.

I say, 'It is easier to make better decisions if you write down assumptions you are making around the decision. Even if your decision doesn't create the intended results, you can go back to see which assumptions you have made wrong.'

Necks are nodding. I wish I could have taken some of my own advice in my life. I break the team into a couple of working groups.

Tina says, 'We discovered something, an unstated assumption as you might call it.'

She gets up and points to the flip chart that reads, *Cipher suits – algorithms.*

'I realised we are making assumptions about the monitoring tool and the way it records information. We will speak to our supplier in Sheffield on this.'

During the break, I empty my bladder. At the urinal, I wonder whether the assumption I am making about my life being a dead end is wrong. Maybe there is hope.

At the end of the meeting, Tina and I stay behind. She closes the door the way Peter did – without a single sound.

She rests her arm on top of the flip chart. 'I'm sorry I haven't been in touch. I assumed you would be busy in your new role. Also, now that you are our supplier, I didn't want to disturb you and take liberties. I know your tech team needs your support.'

I look at the wooden floor. All the planks are polished, without a blemish.

'I didn't thank you enough for the foundations you laid out for our new products. Louis and the juniors mention your methods often. And George says he is still learning a thing or two from you.'

***

After my wedding we went round to endless dinners to meet endless 'uncles' together with Grandad and my parents. Mona had asked me why we were spending so much time analysing our wedding – who got drunk, who avoided who and whether the *bajrachāryas* could have done a better job. After my third dinner, I realised it was all about Grandad and my parents getting heaped with praise for the arrangements. It felt like Mona and I were just mascots for the family.

Right now, though, I want to have a good gossip under the guise of a debrief. In the evening, after everyone is already in bed, I send a message out asking for answers to *What went well at the wedding?* I follow up with *Anything interesting happen?* I save all the messages – some funny, many full of praise – in my Notes app. It will be something to reminisce about when I get old.

Sunita's message says, *Sorry if I was quiet during the whole wedding day. This was my first major occasion without Raff, and I missed him so much.*

I hadn't thought about Raff much on the wedding day, but I know I have a way of pushing things aside. Since the wedding, his memory has surfaced often, but without the same intensity.

A week later, on my return from work, I find four empty cola cans in my front garden. All squashed up. There are two more on my driveway and about another dozen in the neighbour's front patch. I pick them all up and leave them by his front door. I feel like I am returning borrowed toys. John's door opens. He is wearing a vest. He must have heard me rummaging. His arm has two lumps of muscle, and the lower part is rolling with curly hair.

'Hey man, how are you?' He looks at the pile of cans. 'Thanks for doing that.'

His big hands lift them all up in one scoop. He takes one step forward. Recently, I have had two doorstep chats with John. Two days ago, we talked about the bin men being late, the work he is doing on roof repairs and, finally, about his son and his special needs. Yesterday, I borrowed his electronic tyre pump when he noticed my front left tyre was under pressure.

I step towards my door. John takes my cue and nudges open his door with his foot. I can see Nadia's feet at the top of the stairs. Her hair is loose and her face angry. She stands up, runs down and slams the kitchen door.

I turn around to close the door. John shifts his gaze away. He shuts his door in synchronicity with mine.

CHAPTER 10

BALANCE

——————————————

I peek through the red part of the stained-glass kitchen door. Nadia is sitting at the table, hands on her face. That reminds me of sitting in the toilet cubicle at work. My guess is she is in trouble at school or struggling with her tutor. There's a year to go before her GCSEs and we have increased Nadia's tutoring to three hours per week. Last week I had insisted Nadia continue, despite the summer term coming to an end in three weeks.

I stop guessing – my assumptions about the boy next door were so wrong. I turn the handle like I am about to enter a boardroom. Nadia does not move. On the table is an open bag of sea salt crisps. I turn on the instant hot water tap. The pipes creak with the sudden force. My daughter does not flinch. I make half a mug of mint tea and sit on the chair opposite her.

I wonder if problems with that girl at school have resurfaced. I search for my softest voice. 'What's bothering you?'

Her face lifts. She stares at the clock behind my back.

'Dad, I don't need a tutor. I can do it myself. I am confident that I can. My way is so different to hers. She wants me to work on one topic at a time and be clear about what questions might come up in the exam. I must follow the way she wants me to learn … that's crazy, even the teachers at school give you more choices. I like to skim read, then have a chat about it, which kind of … triggers questions I have. After that, I fill in the gaps from possible exam questions.'

She wipes her right eye, even though there are no tears. Her gaze turns on me.

'You remember that girl, Ishita, who I hated?'

I want to say, *How could I forget?*

'Well, we get on fine now and want to work together. We can support each other, kinda act as teachers to each other.'

I want to know how she is now a friend to Ishita.

She fiddles with her hair. Her right-hand palm is prominent.

'Nadia, the GCSEs are important. They will make up a major part of getting an offer from universities.'

She stares at me, her black eyes unflinching. 'You are wasting your money. I told you I don't like the tutor. You told me you need to work things out yourself and not rely on someone pushing you all the time.' She bangs her palm on the table. She says, 'I spoke to *ajī*, and she says if I have a plan for studying, that's enough. I have a plan. I can write it for you.'

Nadia speaking to my mum makes sense. I always turned to Grandad in times of trouble. Sometimes he would not ask questions, just stroke my head. 'What's your plan then?'

Her palm becomes a fist.

'Dad, you said working in a team is important. It worked during the wedding. This is what I want to do for the GCSE mocks. I work one hour after school in the library with Ishita. I come home, relax and then do practice questions at 9 p.m. on the phone every other day, but verbally, no pen involved. Ishita and I have also discussed methods on how we pick things up. In Geography, I always use a template for three areas of food, water and energy for urban and non-urban populations across the world. And Ishita showed me this template called "evidence and argument" to identify change and continuity in History.'

She has me trapped. If Raff was here, he would have said, 'Listen Aman. She has a well-laid-out plan.'

'As for Saturday, Dad, well, I will take it off. And on Sunday, Ishita and I will get together at 2 p.m. and test each other on two subjects.'

I want to argue, but I say, 'Okay, I will temporarily stop the tutoring and we can see how things progress during the year.'

Nadia jumps up. Her face is shining. She gives me a short, tight hug. The next minute, she is on her phone. Her typing is at double speed.

Thursday arrives. It's the evening I most look forward to. Nadia and Nabin are both staying with my mum overnight, with no school due to an INSET day for the teachers. We have a squash court booked for 7 p.m. Mona moves around the court quicker than me. I anticipate many of her shots, but my feet just don't reach in time. She beats me 4–1. Last week, I didn't even win a game. After my shower, I walk across from the sports centre a five-minute walk to the restaurant. The sting of losing games is beginning to fade quicker than usual. Mona arrives ten minutes later. My pint glass of lemonade is empty. We chat about the restaurant décor, followed by the soon-to-be-released detective series on Netflix. When we started dating it was like this; we would flit from topic to topic, making connections to various subjects. The attendant comes three times to see if we have finished. Each time I wave him away. The last slice of pizza is cold on my plate.

We leave at 9:30 p.m. On the way home, we return to the centre reception to get next week's booking in.

The next evening at 8 p.m., I am in the loft. The builder is standing next to me.

He says, 'We can put one large room or two small rooms up, but you will have to lose part of your study room for the build of the stairs.'

I say, 'So, I get a larger room upstairs ... and we lose a room downstairs.'

'I guess that's a good summary.' He gazes at my forehead and says, 'You don't seem so sure about the conversion.'

He scribbles in his notebook and takes more measurements. The total figure with scaffolding, a dormer, labour work, windows, rerouting of heating and electricity comes to £48,500.

As soon as the builder has gone, I start searching for loft designs. My mouse has a life of its own, and by chance, opens the wedding planning folder. Inside, I find a document with the title: *What's not important for the wedding?* Mentally, I remove the word *wedding* and add *house*.

We already have four bedrooms, one each for Nadia and Nabin, plus the study room. Two years ago, the neighbours at no. 47 had done a conversion. They had invited us to have a peek, and Nabin loved it, particularly the ping-pong table.

I scrunch up the builder's quote and put it on the study desk near the computer screen. At the dinner table, no-one asks why the builder had come. At the first quiet moment, I put my fork down. I push my plate an inch forward.

I say, 'I have been thinking about the loft conversion.'

No-one stops munching.

'I'm not sure we need it.'

I pause, waiting for howls. Nabin shrugs. His mouth is full. Mona doesn't stop her motion. Her focus is on wiping off all the chutney from her plate with the garlic bread.

Nadia says, 'I don't remember you mentioning it.'

Straight after dinner, I throw the scrunched-up quote into the bin. It lands perfectly. My head is light. My legs are on the desk, and I settle into the study chair. My phone has the list of repair jobs. In the *done* section are the digital box, the light fitting, the sockets and the garage leak. I glance at the *to do* list of five items, which includes the ivy in the garden and the broken chair. The list is hardly getting shorter. But Nabin and I will have something to do together once a week.

***

The Friday after, I have arranged for Mum to come to our home. I pick up Mum straight from work. She's wrapped Himalayan ginger in a plastic bag, but its pungent citrusy smell has escaped. On the back seat I put her bag of tomatoes and cauliflower for the *tarkārī*. By the time we reach my front door, my mouth is watering. On the driveway, I make her promise to leave the cooking to Mona and me.

Mum had said a week after the wedding, 'One night on Wednesday is enough for bridge. I will miss my Fridays with my friends though. But Nadia is insisting I come to our other home more often.'

I like how we, in our tradition, use the word *our* for any home belonging to a member of the family.

I spread out the cauliflower florets on the worktop. I dislike the shape of cauliflower. It's like something washed out from the stomach. But once it's mashed up you can't see it in *tarkārī*. I chop while Mona does the steaming. My slice of onion has six layers, all individual but tightly packed. George's words about friendship are true. A few months ago, I had just Raff as a friend to talk to. Now I have Lekh, George, Joan and the old lady. And chats with Mona are like when we first met.

I mix the tomatoes, onions, ground cumin and the Himalayan ginger. And add a small pinch of turmeric, red chilli powder and salt. On top, I add the steamed cauliflower and potatoes that Mona has prepared. Mona has a taste. She opens the middle drawer, which has about thirty small jars, and gets the one from the middle of the drawer.

'Nice. Lovely so far, but it needs a bit more cumin.'

I take a sip from the ladle of *tarkārī*. The heat bites my tongue. I gurgle it in my mouth, swallow, and savour the sour spicy taste. It reminds me of my childhood. I must have been nine when my mother once said to Larissa and me, when we were watching her cook, 'Getting the blend right is what taste is about. For that, add the salt and chilli powder last.'

I am at one with the stirring, mesmerised by the bubbling whirl-pool. In the vessel, I sense my family, colleagues, cousins, university friends and even the neighbour. The term *melting pot* is true to me in every way. There is an orange texture; all the vegetables are joined in a union.

I take out some *tarkārī* on the ladle, blowing on the hot steam coming from it. There is no sight of cauliflower; its fused in.

The recipe says to add saffron as a garnish, as an option. I tap my head. We have none. Then from nowhere I see an image of the purple cornflower outside my house.

I want to yell out to my mum. Instead, I say to Mona, 'Can we use the cornflower as a garnish?'

Mona lifts the iPad. She scrolls down and gives me a thumbs up.

'Amazingly, yes. In fact, it's quite common in European dishes. By the way, did you know it was a sign of vitality for the Egyptians?'

I pour the *tarkārī* into a serving bowl. The five petals of purple cornflower look like they are meant to be there, sitting on the orange blend.

We invite Mum to the kitchen as our official taster. Nadia's in tow. Their eyes open wide as we lift the lid to show the *tarkārī*.

Mum takes a sip, letting the *tarkārī* cool in the spoon first. 'It was your grandad who taught me how to improve my *ālū-kāulī tarkārī*. My side of the family could not make it well.'

At dinner we compare the *ālū-kāulī tarkārī* at Kaya's wedding to what's on our plates. My mum seems to have worked out all the subtle differences between the two and the minor differences in ingredients ...

She says, 'Every *tarkārī* is different in each home. That's what makes it a pleasure.'

Nadia's plate is empty within minutes. But she stays at the table making fun of my mum's foibles. During the wedding preparation, I saw the two of them having side chats.

'*Ajī*, can I come to learn how to cook *tarkārī* with you on Tuesdays?'

Mum clutches her hand. That means yes.

Afterwards, I ask Nabin to knock on John's door. He has two plastic boxes with *tarkārī* and rice in his right hand and a supermarket bag with empty tins of tomato purée on his left.

As soon as Nabin lifts the door knocker, I move out of sight but keep the front door open.

John speaks fast. It's the first time we have ever given him any gift. He chats with Nabin for about ten minutes. Nabin explains what the latest football results mean on league positions. John talks about his son's difficulty in Science.

Grandad used to ask me to take leftover food to a single old lady opposite our home in Aldershot when I was eleven. I asked him once why he never came with me. He said, 'You build your own relationships. But come and tell me what the *buḍhī* said to you.'

The pan on the stove is still a third full. There are enough servings left for four people.

I say to Mona, 'Shall we freeze this and give this to Lekh whenever we see him next?'

She smiles and nods. She writes on the box *Tarkārī – LP*. Lekh's house is a seventy-minute drive, but now that's not far away. My grandad once said to Lekh and me, 'A cousin can become your best friend ... you already have many things in common to build on.'

I switch on my screen and connect the video call. Larissa wants to see us all, even though it is past midnight in Mauritius. I ask Mum if she can hear the sea waves from the speaker. Larissa's background is bright with her spotlights. But there are dark patches under her eyes. By any measure, she has all her needs taken care of. She has no money issues, lives on a beautiful island and just passed a momentous milestone of her daughter's wedding.

'What's happening?' I ask.

She says nothing for a minute and then says, 'Work is hell, but I don't want to talk about it.'

I want to say, *Good life is not about your pāgal career.*

She waves to Mona. 'I want to know all about the new *tarkārī* recipe. It looked bright orange in the photo you sent.'

I have never seen her face so puffed up. Yet, I know that as soon as another opportunity comes, she will bounce back. And her calls will get less frequent. I read through the six handwritten 'thank you' messages from the wedding. Her lips curl up, and her eyes are no longer squinting.

***

I have an interview set up with a start-up company. The founder is five years younger than me and has a small team there. I have discovered that most of his staff are technology graduates with three or four years of experience.

Our initial meeting is at the Institute of Electrical Engineers, in their members' lounge. The place is decorated with sculptures and busts of famous engineers, and I pass a panelled library on our way up to the second floor. Some of the world's top history engineers were Italian and British, and Joan told me that many Renaissance artists were inspired by logic and maths.

He says, 'I won't bore you with technical and management questions.' He taps on his laptop. 'I am sure you are well versed in this. So, tell me what motivates you?'

His hands are twitching just like mine. I decide not to spew out bullshit.

'Well, I am a bit stuck where I am. Plus, I have a high need to prove myself, something from my background … you know, upbringing. I think I will like the environment of a start-up.'

He laughs and then nods, and then goes through the role in more detail. 'I am also talking to someone you know – Joan Preston – for another role. If you are okay, I'd like to arrange a meeting with both of you so that we can discuss plans together. Please bear with me, as I line up things.'

So Joan was behind this interview. I want to beg him to take me on straight away. Instead, I nod like it all makes sense.

At our next meeting, Joan is with us. We meet in an office with just two floors. On the first floor is a row of six desks and two medium-sized meeting rooms. Yet, I don't feel claustrophobic. Their location is two tube stops away from DigiArt. Striking distance of both Zeno's café and my favourite park. We are in the meeting room for four hours.

He asks me during the break if I have any general questions. I prepared for this. 'What are your company values? There is nothing in the documents so far, nor a section in the business plan.'

He closes his eyes for a few seconds. 'We don't have any written values. It's easy to make something up, but I don't want to. If you want the answer just spend a bit more time with the rest of the team.'

At least he is not making things up.

Joan says, 'I had a wander round earlier. I got a sense of flow, support and curiosity.' She looks at me. 'I guess company culture is like a painting, it can't be understood by someone else's words. Inter-action will give you a direct feeling.'

I like this kind of philosophical talk.

***

A week later, Joan and I sign our employment contracts. My pay is a bit more than what I get on the second floor, but I don't bother to calculate the exact percentage. Anyway, my loft conversion is cancelled. I have zero plans for a foreign holiday. On top of that, I have no standing order for tutor fees.

Joan tells me afterwards that she is taking a large cut and that after two years of funding, there is uncertainty for this start-up.

But I never want to be back on that second floor. Having a dead-end job caused me more anxiety than the uncertainty of having this one.

We head together to the BDG meeting which starts at 6 p.m.

I say on the tube, 'We should be saying a prayer to Botticelli, our god, for the opportunity.'

She laughs and says, 'Why don't you do a talk on Botticelli and how his paintings are being incorporated digitally? Like in the fashion industry.'

My mind freezes. All I can say is, 'Maybe.'

At 6:30, Joan stands up to introduce the talk. She adds, 'We have a slot available for our next session. Aman is going to do what I know will be a fascinating talk on how Botticelli's work is being used in our modern world from fashion to fusion. Thank you, Aman, for volunteering.'

My heart rate is beating so hard, it might miss a beat. I stroke the temple of my head and then brush my hair. Speaking in front of these experts would be something special.

***

That evening, I scroll through old messages from friends and relatives. The last call from Kaya was two days after the wedding. Since then, we haven't had a proper conversation, just three short messages.

My hand hovers over the green button under her name, but I withdraw my thumb. I have done my job and my duties. Grandad would be proud. Family will always be around.

Mona sends me a message the next day: *Don't forget it's Lekh's birthday today.* It's 1:30 p.m. On impulse, I call him.

'I am glad you called. I was going to ask you for some advice on buying a self-driving car.'

Lekh hasn't changed his car, the Toyota, for ten years.

I forward him the animated digital card from BMW, which is gold with a silver heading. It says, *Exclusive launch event for Mr Pradhan and guest at our Park Lane showroom.* I write with the card, *Seriously expensive cars, but it will be good fun to poke around.*

A week later, we are eyeing every detail of the two navy blue cars on display. The larger car has what I expect: no pedals, just a handbrake and a small steering wheel. The new laws came out early this year. This means that on motorways and most A roads, there is no need to be at the steering wheel ... The salesman sees me reading the literature.

'In case you are wondering, the control is both with the car computer and the national highway. They have a well-developed

AI computer. It can stop the car in three seconds, with its immense ability to track potential problems.'

He opens the car and waves his arm like an usher. 'The seats in the front can turn around, and a small table can pop out from the floor in between.'

I touch the twin dashboards. 'But how can you be sure that the AI will work in all circumstances, particularly on an urban road that may have more dangers?'

He twists out of the car. His black shoes sparkle in the bright artificial light. 'We are sure; it's been tested in all conditions and all eventualities.'

'What about a crazy dog crossing?' I wish I could use the word *pāgal* for *crazy* to impress Lekh.

He frowns but his voice is confident. 'Yes, it takes care of all situations, even animal-related hazards.'

I respond, 'But you can't guarantee that, can you?'

'BMW have tested these cars in all situations.'

He stands up. I decide not to push him any further; he is just a salesman.

I say to Lekh out of earshot, 'Circumstances will occur that no AI car can cope with. Human drivers have the advantage due to our ability to solve unforeseen and even abstract problems.'

Lekh nods twice, like he did when we agreed on things as kids. But he has all three brochures in his hand. We go to the nearest coffee shop.

Lekh says, 'I'm planning my next trip to Nepal, probably November. It may be the last chance to visit *Hajurābubā*. He will be ninety-one next month. Why don't you join me?'

Lekh's posture is a copy of Raff's. Arms open and a look of certainty.

I want to say yes. Instead, I say, 'What sort of things do you do when you're out there? See the Himalayas, go trekking?'

He shakes his head. 'Won't do much. Spend time meeting folks and just being there.'

I see myself in Kathmandu relaxing without a care in the world. I hear myself saying 'Okay, I am in.'

***

The Friday after, I start clearing my desk. I have already lost my access rights to our art storage systems. It's a pity, as I wanted to have one last browse. At noon, I am summoned to the fourth floor. There is a small gathering arranged by Louis and George to wish me goodbye. The CEO is there, as are Tina and Emily.

The CEO says, 'Aman played a fundamental part in our new products; his talents are going to be useful for the company he is going to.'

I have a digital card on a scrolling screen with gushing comments on each page. On the small round table is a medium-sized wrapped gift. I play along. Louis makes some gushing comments and Tina pats my shoulder. Emily puts my gift in a cloth bag embossed with a Titian painting. All pleasant, but I don't want to be here for even one more second.

***

Three days later, I am driving north on the M1. The car boot is almost full. Not squeezing everything into rectangular bags for flights is a relief. In late August, the peak temperature is always over 27°C. I am armed with some knowledge from a borrowed book from Kishan. Its title is *Joy of the Peak District*. As we pass Buxton in Derbyshire, we see huge lakes with small pebbly beaches. Nadia and Nabin put their devices on the seat and gaze from the right window. The forests remind me of our expensive trip to Sri Lanka three years ago. We had paid a tour guide hefty money for a guided walk in the jungle.

My grandad had said in the year he died, 'Everything you want is sometimes near, you just need to look harder to find it.'

On our first day, we visit a place called Padley Gorge, a shallow valley with a bubbling stream and rocks. Two families are sitting just above the stream, having a break during their walk. A thick forest overhangs behind them. There are wispy clouds above, moving slowly. The flowers on our left are of a pure white.

I snap a picture and send it to Joan with the message, *One guess at what painter this reminds you of?*

She responds straight away. *Constable! Are you enjoying the countryside, Aman?*

On the third day, we embark on a six-mile walk in a signposted forest between two hills. A third of the way through, my left knee starts hurting with every step. It's dark. My head is up. There are a few small spots of blue, the rest is a green canopy. Many roots are running across the ground on the forest floor. They all seem connected, creating some sort of web. The rest of the family are twenty metres in front of me and stop.

'Oh my god, look at this wild apple tree. The apples are huge!' says Nadia. She plucks one and takes a bite.

Nabin starts picking the larger ones and fills up our bag.

I stand still, my right foot on a ground root. There are popping images coming to my mind: Botticelli's paintings, the mountains in Nepal and the head of the Buddha, Kaya's wedding. They are emerging from the roots, appearing and disappearing on the forest floor. My head feels light. I kneel and touch a root. I want to become part of it.

'Dad, come and help me get these apples. Mum is going to make chutney with them when we get home.' Nabin taps my shoulder, and I stand up straight. The images disappear.

On our last morning, my eyes open at 7:35 a.m. For the first time in years, I can't recall a single dream. I don't think I had one. Nothing is whizzing in my mind. I make a pot of mint tea and Mona appears a few minutes later. We are both sitting side by side at the oak kitchen table. I hear a bird chirping at the same beat as the clock ticking on the back door. From the large window by the sink, I can see two V-shaped hills and a valley beyond. Mona puts her hand on my thigh. I stroke her palm.

I say, 'The Peak District is two and a half hours away from home. It cost us £20 for the EV charge. That's half the price of a taxi to the airport for our Sri Lanka trip.'

She squeezes my hand. She says, 'And the beauty is as nice as any of our foreign holidays.'

I point out some of the undulating features from the window. I get the urge to buy a painting.

I find on my device a Constable replica of the painting called *The Cornfield*. We both gaze at it. It's like the view from yesterday's walk. It has two woods, a stream and the sight of a small village. The cost is £350. Mona doesn't resist. I see it as an investment. I will put it on the landing next to *Mars and Venus*.

✳✳✳

A few days into my new job, I see a message about Louis on LinkedIn: *Congratulate Louis on his promotion – Manager of Product Development, DigiArt.*

I have a tenseness in the pit of my stomach. I put a single 👏 and try not to read the gushing comments. I curse at myself and start typing, *Louis, you will excel in this role.* The tenseness in my pit reduces.

He contacts me via a WhatsApp message later in the afternoon: *I came to this country in hope, which turned into misery. I was even homeless for a while. So many people have helped me, including you.*

On Friday, the founder sends me five CVs. His message says: *A Cloud support role for the new platform. Can you do the final shortlist and send it to me please?*

The second CV has the name Annetta Kowalski at the top in a large black font. The top paragraph says, *I have just completed my MicroMasters in Cloud Computing Architecture.* She has talked about her experience at the coffee shop like I had asked her to. Grandad's words echo in my mind: 'Sometimes you may meet someone in your life again in a surprising way. That's not just by chance, it's because of fate. Relationships happen for a reason.'

I use the green digital pen and colour in her name on the PDF. I add my comment in next to her name: *She comes across well. Yes for an interview.*

Joan, the founder and I are an intensive team, but it's like working with friends not workmates. My time at DigiArt is now becoming a blur. The founder has high standards, but he doesn't hide his human frailties.

Yesterday, during a break, he told me about a panel in his kitchen he couldn't take off, until his ten-year-old pointed out the hidden screws underneath the wooden cap.

He had laughed and said, 'No matter how intelligent we are, we can be blind to many things.'

I had replied spontaneously, 'The Buddha has said that not living in each moment makes us blind.'

Only Emily knew about my faith in my last job.

One Tuesday afternoon, I am in the middle of a workshop with the technical team. The founder is also there. My phone vibrates. It's Kaya. In the past, I would have been annoyed. This time I move towards the door.

'I need to take an urgent call from a family member,' I say.

I expect annoyance. Everyone nods their head in unison.

Kaya says, 'I haven't forgotten you, *māmā*.'

I like being called *māmā*.

'Been busy … so many things to organise in married life. Anyway, Nadia's birthday is coming up in September and I want to arrange a surprise. I wanted to fix a date.'

We fix the 27th of September, and I fire a message to Mona. And then I invite Lekh, his family and *kākā*. There is a tear in my right eye. I wait for it to dry before heading back.

***

One day, in late September, Joan is not at work. She is on leave to spend time with her mum. I have picked up some of her commercial work. The clock on my screen says 1:50 p.m. I haven't had lunch. I need to finalise two contracts by tomorrow.

I get a text from George at 2:10 p.m.: *Hope you are still on for our meet. See you at 2.30 – George* 😇.

I push the lid down on my laptop.

He is already there when I arrive. He has a pot with the strings of two teabags hanging out of it. He puts his hand in his pocket and takes out two tiny transparent packets.

'I got you this from the seeds germinating in my shed. Grow it in a large pot and you should get some all year round. Mizuna – an Eastern salad.'

I don't ask a single question about the politics at DigiArt. I'm not even curious. George does the talking, stopping periodically to get acknowledgement. He goes through the best types of salads to grow in a pot and his voluntary role with abandoned animals. He doesn't share a single thing about work. I study him: his face, gestures and tone. He looks different but I don't know why. Then it hits me. What I can see now is George, the whole human in one, not filtered by my bias of him from work. Raff would approve of my new friendship.

The park is on the way back to the tube station. I enter via the middle gate nearest to the bench where I used to sit, hoping to see the old lady. It's been many weeks now. There are around twenty people in the park. Mainly dog walkers, a few mothers with prams and a father teaching his toddler to walk. It's quieter than when I last came. I can't see any birds. On the right is a mulberry bush, which is still in full bloom. From this angle, the park trees appear bunched – a resemblance of the Peak District. I take a photo and send it to Mona. I have two contracts to finish but no desire to leave. I look at the many clouds in the sky and try to spot some meaningful shapes. That was my favourite hobby when I was six. I see the shape of an elephant's trunk and a broken but large bracelet from the cirrus clouds. And a shape of a mountain in Nepal or maybe a hill in the Peak District. I scan the horizon, and the west has a tinge of ultramarine blue.

From the distance, via the car park entrance, I recognise the walking stick – a distinctive stripy brown. But she is not on her own. I am over to her, almost running.

She sees me approaching and stops. She turns around and points her stick to the person next to her. She elongates my name, 'Amaaan, this is Joan, my daughter.'

Joan gives me a wink. She thrusts out her hand. I giggle, which breaks into a laugh. She must have known all along about my chats with her mum. Her mum can't stand straight. But she shares many features with Joan: the high cheekbones, the silken hair and the oval eyes.

Joan points to the nearest bench. I sit in the middle of them.

The old lady says, 'I have just come out of hospital. It's so wonderful to see you again. They say my pancreas needs a lot of care. Last time we spoke, you were trapped on the second floor?' She snorts and shows her dentures. 'Have you escaped from that place?'

After a few minutes, the old lady glances at Joan. I hold her hand and help her up. She squeezes my palm and lets go. She starts to shuffle towards the gate leading to the car park.

Joan comes close and whispers near my ear, 'From my mum's description, I thought it was you. But wasn't 100% sure. She described you as a handsome man from the Himalayas.'

I stand and watch them until they are at the park's edge. I put my hand on my chest. It's warm and thudding.

As I walk back from the park to the tube station, at the zebra crossing, there are two self-driving cars. One has no passengers. In the other, there is a couple tapping away on their phones. I keep my eyes on the cars as I cross, waiting for a careless move. I don't trust technology fully, not yet.

***

Eight days later, I get a text from Joan. It says, *Mum died yesterday. I won't be in the office for another week at least.*

A day after, she sends me a WhatsApp message: *I found this poem in Mum's living room.*

The attached photo reads:

To Aman, Love from Edith (lady in Bellflower Park!)
Life is like balancing on a many-legged see-saw,
With friends and foes tugging, pushing us raw.
Join the dots of your life carefully,
Whether at home, office, park or gallery.
Amidst weeds, flowers bloom and grow,
As surrounding trees stand tall, a sight to behold.
Your life will never be at ease,
Yet, like a painter, you must make it complete.
What you do may not matter to anyone in the end,
Yet, some power is there, that comprehends.

www.ingramcontent.com/pod-product-compliance
Lightning Source LLC
Chambersburg PA
CBHW031303120726
47906CB00003B/861